THE

VIRTUAL WORLD

D1553372

VIRTUAL WORLD

BY CHRIS WESTWOOD

VIKING

VIKING
Published by the Penguin Group
Penguin Putnam Inc., 375 Hudson Street, New York, New York 10014, U.S.A.
Penguin Books Ltd, 27 Wrights Lane, London W8 5TZ, England
Penguin Books Australia Ltd, Ringwood, Victoria, Australia
Penguin Books Canada Ltd, 10 Alcorn Avenue, Toronto, Ontario, Canada M4V 3B2
Penguin Books (N.Z.) Ltd, 182-190 Wairau Road, Auckland 10, New Zealand

Penguin Books Ltd, Registered Offices: Harmondsworth, Middlesex, England

First published in Great Britain in 1996 by Penguin Books Ltd.
First published in the United States of America in 1997 by Viking, a member of
Penguin Putnam Inc.

1   3   5   7   9   10   8   6   4   2

LIBRARY OF CONGRESS CATALOGING-IN-PUBLICATION DATA
Westwood, Chris.
Virtual world / by Chris Westwood.
p.   cm.
Summary : Fourteen-year-old Jack North finds himself literally
drawn into the frightening world of what he thinks is a new virtual
reality game.
ISBN 0-670-87546-5
[1. Virtual reality—Fiction.   2. Computers—Fiction.   3. Science
fiction.]   I. Title
PZ7.W5274Vi   1997   [Fic]—dc21   97-9388   CIP   AC

Printed in U.S.A.
Set in Frutiger Roman

We have to get our facts straight, even when we're dealing in make-believe, so I'd like to give thanks to the global community known as the Internet, which is where many of the technical facts and figures for this novel were gleaned. Since there were somewhere between thirty and forty million Net users at the last count, I'm sure you'll understand if I don't thank each one individually.

A round of applause, too, must go to my editor Lucy Ogden—and of course many others at Penguin, all of whom may well know who they are—for patiently waiting . . . and waiting . . . throughout the two years *Virtual World* took to complete. It was a long haul, but we got there in the end!

It wasn't all hard graft of course. For example, I idled away too many hours playing games on my Mac and running up huge phone bills on-line, but the time and expense were well worth it, because I learned so many new things about our world: how truly vast and varied and downright wacky it can sometimes be. I hope this comes through when you read what follows. If it does, then I've done my job. Your part of the bargain is to imagine the rest. . . .

All the best,

cw@shock.demon.co.uk

BINARY FICTION

CHAPTER ONE

In hyperspace, he was king. Whenever he sensed the adversary closing in near the border of Zone Eleven, Jack North kicked up a gear, scattered a freight load of pyro mines in his wake like confetti, hit the Escape key, and fled. Behind him, the Agents of Darkness were toast.

Invincible, he thought. *I'm invincible.* But it hadn't always been so. Sure, he had been born with talent, a keen eye, and razor-sharp reflexes, but talent alone meant nothing unless your nerves were steel-plated, too. A good and steady nerve was vital if you intended to stay alive, let alone win the war. Now, dipping low to avoid the airborne scanners on the outer continent, serpentining through a black space of acid geysers, he was coasting.

"Jack?"

The voice came from somewhere outside himself. Hardly recognizing it, he grunted at the distraction. The geysers were history now and he was homing in on the mission objective. A chromium gateway glittered some distance ahead on the route to Zone Seven. It looked like the entrance to a palace, except that there was nothing beyond the entrance itself, only the archway and the magenta and blue horizon. Once through the arch, he'd be home and dry. It should

3

have been a walkthrough, but the gateway was flanked by two mean-minded battle cruisers of purple and yellow—a hot, harsh color combination that made him all the more eager to zap them. Around him the air snapped with angry fire. He could feel the heat on his cheeks.

Jack raised the shields.

"Jack? Jack? Where are you?"

Again the voice, but he was too lost to care or acknowledge. It must be his mother, calling from somewhere downstairs, he guessed. She couldn't know how critically poised the new mission was, how costly a moment's indecision could be. Flack peppered the outer shell of his vessel. White lights rippled like dying stars just yards away, filling the view screen with static. One of the battlecruisers—huge and diamond shaped—made a sudden upward surge toward him, but then wandered stupidly into his sights.

You're gone, son.

In one fluent series of actions, Jack dipped, took aim, double-clicked, and watched the cruiser roll off into the night, smoldering, irreversibly broken. As it hit the ground, a yellow-black fireball lit up the landscape below.

Now, he thought. *Now. Down, down, down.*

The second cruiser still blocked his path. Jack's vessel rocked as the cruiser's artillery half-drained his shields. A red LED on the control console registered the damage level: sixty percent. Worse, he reckoned, was the fact that he now had only 10 or 15 percent ammunition in hand, and the nearest recharge site was many minutes away, even at warp speed. Another tremor. Damage levels approaching over-load. The cruiser reared up in his sights, and—

"Jack?"

"Not now!" He sounded angry; felt angry, but that was because the damage he'd sustained could cost him the game. In spite of this he was flowing, and the first rule of combat was that the flow must never be broken. One brief lapse could spell disaster. Nothing was over until it was over. Swiveling the control to his right, double-clicking, double-clicking again, he drew a broad arc around the cruiser, un-loaded the last of his scatter mines, and with wide, astonished green eyes saw the thing swallowed up by a crater five times its own size.

Then: through the gateway, one quick rush of adrenaline, and he was home, safe and sound. Bells rang out. Chimes chimed. Jack covered his face for a moment, catching his breath. The final bright explosion was still impressed some-where in the brown dark beneath his eyelids. It took several more moments before he sensed he had company.

Kyle Hallaway was at the door, clucking his tongue as he stepped inside the room, shaking his head slowly back and forth as he peered across Jack's shoulder at the shimmering screen. He wore faded jeans and a white, oil-smeared T-shirt with the logo I HAVE NO MOUTH AND I MUST SCREAM under his flying-jacket.

"Should've known," he said lightly. "They've been calling

you for ages, your mum and your sis. Sandy said I should just come straight up. In fact she said you ought to get your butt in gear. Her exact words. You should listen to what your big sister says." Then, after a pause, "You still playing this piece of old junk?"

"Junk?" Jack glared, swiveling round in his second-hand office chair. "Just look at these scores, you animal." He gestured at the screen where his ratings read:

```
TACTICS: A1
RISK: A1
AGGRESSION: LOOK OUT!
CONTROL: CRUCIAL
```

"That's yesterday's thing," Kyle said, making himself at home, sprawling leisurely on Jack's bed. Once upon a time, he would have said last year's thing, but life moved at such a clip these days, time stood still for no man. Fast-forward or dead stop were your only real options. Sweeping up a model of the *Enterprise Mk V* from the nightstand next to the bed, Kyle wriggled upright against the headboard to admire it. "That shoot-'em-up stuff is for the museums. Does Silicon Sphere mean anything to you?"

Jack didn't need to consider. "The new interactive game?"

"If that's what you want to call it." Kyle replaced the *Enterprise* model on its stand, ran his fingers back like a comb through his thick mop of wiry, black hair. "That's tomorrow's thing, that is."

"I know, I know." Jack knew only too well. He'd been salivating over the rumors of Silicon Sphere long enough. "Everyone's talking about it, but just talking. I haven't heard of anyone who's actually tried it yet, apart from the magazines, but they don't seem to know much either. I bet it's going to cost more than I can afford."

"Not necessarily." Kyle grinned and formed strange moving shapes with his lips. A ray of mischievous light had entered his eyes. "What would you say if I told you I could give you a piece of tomorrow . . . today?"

"How so?"

"Supposing I knew someone who knew someone who—"

"Get to the point," Jack told him impatiently.

"There are rumors," Kyle said, "that copies started circulating the Net yesterday or the day before. I haven't seen it myself yet, but—"

"But Sphere is commercial stuff, isn't it? It's definitely not shareware."

Kyle grinned. "Really, Jack, you ought to know better: we all know the Net's crawling with pirated software. No one's crazy enough to leave stuff like that hanging around in one place for very long, but you'll sure as hell find it on the binary news groups if you keep looking." The binary groups were those which received postings of software as well as messages. A number of these had been outlawed for years, but cyberspace was still hard to police. You could never out-hack the hackers.

"Which groups would they be?" Jack asked.

7

"It hardly matters now. One major snag, Jack. I heard that our local news server crashed sometime last night and took about 80,000 or so messages with it."

"Damn it all. So where does that leave us? Don't tell me someone you know actually got their hands on the thing."

"You're quick. In fact, fingers crossed, he'll be sending a copy tonight. Our very own Roy McKee, no less."

"You're kidding."

"I kid you not." Kyle's grin was widening by the second.

Jack North let out an appreciative whistle. This was great news; news he'd hardly dared hope for. "But what do you really know about the game?" he wondered. The magazines had raved and drooled, but had disclosed precious little about Sphere, except that it was a must. Of course, the less you were allowed to know the more you wanted to. Everyone loved a dark secret, and from all accounts Silicon Sphere held more secrets than most.

"From what I hear," Kyle said, rolling his lanky frame from the bed and crossing the room to lift Jack's virtual reality visor from its place on his desk, "it leaves all this standing. VR? Yesterday's thing!"

"Oh really!"

"No kidding. This, and that—" He waved a hand at the still-shimmering monitor and strapped the visor over his eyes. "—it'll look like old hat next to this new thing."

"Did you just come here to insult me?" Jack wondered.

"Of course. Why else would I want to see you?"

Jack threw a mock punch. In true VR style, still wearing the visor, Kyle dodged it. "No, not really," he said at last. "I came to take you away from all this. We're going to Roy McKee's place for that download. So put your damn mouse away and get moving."

CHAPTER TWO

The mail log on Roy McKee's screen read something like this:

```
--Transcript of session follows--
While talking to relay1.unex.net:
>>RCPT To:> gsharp@nwu.edu>
<<550 <gs@nwu.edu>...User unknown
--Internet Message Header Follows--
Received: from mailgate.jnet.com (lapsang)
by jnet.com with SMTP id AA072628
(5.65c8/IDA-1.4.4 for <Roy
McKee@Zonkers.alpha.co.uk@exnet.com>);
Fri, 18 May 02:41:10 +0100
Received: from jnet.com (assam.jnet.com)
by mail-gate.jnet.com id AA104073
(5.65c/IDA-1.4.4); Fri, 18 May 02:40:55
+0100
Date: Fri, 18 May 02:40:55+0100
From: Mail Delivery Subsystem <MAILER-
FAUST@lapsang>
Message-Id: <169405170140.AA102063@
mailgate. jnet.com>
To: <Roy McKee@zonkers.alpha.co.uk>
Cc: Postmaster@lapsang
Subject: Returned mail: User unknown
```

"Meaning what?" Kyle said. "Meaning what exactly? Will someone please explain what's going on?"

Roy leaned way back in his chair, adjusting his rimless glasses. "Well, there's a communication breakdown somewhere, but I just can't figure it out. Here's the message I sent." In a flash he had it scrolling up the screen. "See? A simple request for file transfer. Greg Sharp—GS in this transcript—is the whiz kid in the U.S. I've been trading software with. He's a student at Northwestern University and he's got a direct Net connection through the school which is how I heard about Silicon Sphere. See here." He double-clicked on an archived message, bringing it up on the screen. "This e-mail came in yesterday."

```
Hi Roy,
I hear someone just put Sphere on-line.
Haven't seen it myself, but will be doing a
search later on. Interested? I'll bet! Let
me know anyway.
:-)
G.
```

"So you e-mailed Greg to say go ahead," Kyle said, "but the message never got through." He looked long and hard at Jack, shaking his head. "Can't you try again?"

Roy shrugged. "I could, but look, the report says, 'user unknown.' Now what does that mean? User unknown, for crying out loud. The system couldn't locate him. I've been mailing Greg for a year now. This never happened before."

"Can't you phone him?"

"If you'll pay for it. This isn't like logging on to Alpha, remember." Alpha was the local service provider, twelve miles away, which provided basic Internet services—mail and news, Web access—for the cost of a local call. "On second thought, no you can't. I don't have his number."

"You've been corresponding with this kid for a year and you don't have his number?"

"Only his e-mail address."

"So what now?" Kyle was as uptight as a cat on hot tiles. "People don't just disappear from the Net. If he'd moved he would've left a forwarding address. Where the hell is he?"

Roy sat drumming the desktop with his fingers. "Here, let me try something else. Greg has this friend at Northwestern who runs a VR conference on the Net. I'll try him. He might know something." For ten or twelve seconds his fingers blurred over the keyboard as he typed:

```
To: billwallis@nwu.edu

Billy,
What on earth's happened to Greg? He's sup-
posed to be forwarding me a copy of Sphere
tonight. No record of him at nwu. Relay said,
"User unknown." Any clues?
Regards,
Roy
```

After sending the message, he logged off. "If this doesn't work, I don't know what to tell you. We'll just have to buy the thing when it's released. Now all we can do is wait."

Other people still watched TV, so having e-mailed the message through Alpha they huddled in the pale, antiseptic living room sipping coffee while Roy's old man skipped channels with a small gray remote. Roy's mother had left home last year for a broker or some such high-flyer, and his father hadn't taken it too well overall. He was prone to bouts of anger and depression these days, and it was always better to keep on the right side of him, Jack had learned. After a time the old man fixed on the shopping channel and began browsing through the offers on gardening equipment, though none of the apartments in the complex had gardens or access to gardens except for a concrete atrium. He began gnawing his lip as he tapped his credit card number into the remote control pad to buy something he'd seen, then changed his mind, aborted, and switched to a list of on-line movies instead.

"New toy?" Jack observed.

"Yeah." Roy's father was still transfixed by the screen. "Still can't get used to it. I'm not sure I like the idea of my personal details floating around on some wire somewhere."

"You still buy that way, though," Roy said. "You could always take a hike to the hypermarket."

"As if I have any choice. Just look at the state of my legs. I can't get around the way I used to."

To Jack, Tom McKee's legs looked perfectly okay. They carried him to the kitchen easily enough whenever he needed another beer from the fridge, for example. He couldn't have been more than forty or forty-five anyway. He was a hypochondriac, good and proper.

"What's wrong with you all?" he said after a lull. "How old are you? Fourteen or fifteen? Shouldn't you be out with girls instead of doing whatever it is you do up there on that machine?"

"Girls? What're they?" Kyle wondered.

"You know what I'm saying. Why don't you all get a life?"

"Look who's talking," Roy countered before he could stop himself. "I mean, at least we're in touch with other people. People all over the world. You just sit here alone, eating junk food and feeling sorry for yourself. No offense."

"I'll speak to you later. I won't embarrass you here in front of your friends." His gaze shifted from the TV to fix, unsteadily, on Jack. "You'll have to excuse my son. He has the manners of a drop-out."

"I know he loves me, really," Roy said quickly.

"The point I'm trying to make is, in my day—"

"Uh oh. Here we go. In my day . . ." Roy was struggling not to laugh.

"In my day we used to go out. We'd walk across fields, fish in the rivers and streams, or take a nice girl to the movies. We'd read books. Remember books? But what do

14

you do?" He was staring at Roy, bewildered. "Why can't you try some of those things?"

It was Kyle who answered first. "There *are* no fields anymore. Not around here, anyway. You have to get a bus way out. And the waterways are polluted with gunk, and the theater went out of business aeons ago, ever since movies went on-line. Besides, the streets belong to the gangs, so where does that leave us?"

"Doesn't it make you angry? Don't you reckon you're missing out?"

Kyle shook his head. "Don't know. What you've never had you never miss."

"That's sad. Really sad. But there *are* still girls, aren't there? I don't think they've gone out of style. You should try talking to one sometime. You might be pleasantly surprised."

"The older generation," Roy murmured, getting up. "Don't you just love 'em?"

"He has a point, though," Jack said, shadowing Roy back to his room, minutes later. "I've seen photos of Newton when we used to have fields, trees, even horses and sheep. My folks grew up here and kept piles of snapshots on disk. It looked great. It's hardly recognizable now."

"The old man isn't getting at *us*," Roy explained, back at the console. "He's just moping. If you knew him, you'd understand. I guess he just wishes things were better for us, but how would we know if things were worse now than they used to be?"

Jack considered. He had been born, three months short of fifteen years ago, in a tall, gray highrise with views on all sides of other even taller highrises. To the northwest, where today a maze of sixty-four interlinked highway lanes pulsated with traffic around the clock, there had once been a lake and a green tree horizon. All of this his father had captured on 35 millimeter film before archiving the shots on CD. It still amazed Jack, studying the very earliest images, how much like Sandy his mother had seemed back then, in her early twenties; the same pale oval face, the same stunning auburn hair. There were even a few stills of himself, about three years old, building castles in the sand on an east-coast beach. The sand looked vaguely gray and discolored. The last time he'd been there the beach had a black, oily sheen.

Twenty minutes later, when Roy logged on for the third time, a reply to his message was waiting. This was a stroke of good fortune; Bill Wallis must have been on-line when the item was sent. Sometimes a reply could take hours to arrive through the slow local relay traffic, sometimes days.

"Gotcha," Kyle screamed as Roy clicked open his mailbox, then opened the following from America:

```
Hey Roy⌐
Good   timing.   Something's   up⌐   because   I
can't  seem  to  get  Greg  by  e-mail  or  phone.
He's  always  in  about  now.  I'll  check  again
later.  The  waster's  probably  lost  in  the
game.  Don't  know  about  user  unknown  though.
```

16

> I'll check that for you too. I've uploaded
> Sphere for you anyway.

And there it was. A small gray icon at the foot of Bill's message was labeled: *Attached File: Silicon Sphere.hqx.* Roy double-clicked on the icon and a small 3D progress box on the screen began monitoring the transfer. It was a large file, over thirteen megabytes fully compressed, and would take six or seven minutes to arrive.

Kyle prowled the room while the download took place. Every now and then he flashed an anxious glance at the screen, checked his watch, picked up a book from one of Roy's shelves—*A Clockwork Orange*—then put it back without opening it. By the time Roy had finished transferring copies onto DAT tapes, he was practically sweating.

Jack had never seen Kyle so on edge, not even during last semester's exams. He had seen him uptight, excitable, and just plain overbearing, but never so intense as this. It was almost as if he knew something about the game that no one else did.

CHAPTER THREE

On the bus home, Kyle kept dragging the DAT copy Roy had given him from a pocket to study it as if in sheer disbelief. His long hair fell over his eyes so that his face was unreadable.

"It's only a game," Jack said.

Kyle remained absolutely still, but said nothing. His lips were pursed, unsmiling, his body tense. He didn't nod or shake his head. As the bus doors swished open on Schaefferstown Street he muttered something that Jack couldn't make out for the noise outside. From somewhere in the middle distance, probably over in the Riverside quarter, came a sound of muffled, continuous gunshots. The sound cut off as the doors closed again. Riverside had become a no-go zone in less than two years, ever since the town planners decided to shoehorn all the problem families into it. It was only a matter of time, Jack's father was fond of saying, before the war broke out of the shantytown. Sweeping the problem out of sight would not make it vanish.

"What did you say?" Jack asked.

Kyle looked at him. "Just that you're right. It *is* only a game. But I think it's the one we've been waiting for. How's it feel to hold the future in your hands?"

Jack shrugged and scrambled his own tape out. It felt like any tape; any storage medium. There was nothing so sacred or strange about it. "Good. But I can't figure out why you're so—"

"Why I'm so *what*?" Kyle interrupted. "It isn't like it's got a hold on me." *But it has,* Jack thought. "How many conferences on Usenet have you read lately where Sphere hasn't been the main topic of conversation? Everyone's asking about it. Everyone's hungry to know more. And the more you wonder, the more it intrigues you. You have to admit it's got to you, too."

Jack couldn't deny it, but what he saw in Kyle was different somehow. It verged on obsession. He remembered the first time Kyle got his hands on a second-hand virtual reality visor, and how for weeks afterwards he'd raved to the point of boring anyone who'd listen to him. He'd made similar noises a month or so before the release of *Digital Domain,* a bog-standard 3D shoot-'em-up, but as always his interest had waned even before he'd cracked the top game-playing level.

He was easily thrilled and easily bored, was Kyle. He'd been born with an attention span of about six milliseconds, which had shortened dramatically over the years. But, still, this was different. This time, he was hooked before he'd even got started.

Kyle hopped off the bus at Niven Street, saying good night with no more than a nod and a grunt. Jack watched through the window while he wandered away, hardly look-

19

ing where he was going; a tall black shape caught in a cross-blaze of neon outside McDonald's and Woolworth and Software City, still cradling the tape in his hands like a treasured pet.

It was the start of the weekend now, and from Kyle's point of view the timing couldn't be better. Tonight Kyle would creep into his folks' house, grab a bite from the fridge and vanish into his room until Monday.

Not me, though, Jack thought. *No, not me.*

Oh yeah?

The DAT tape felt snug and secure in his pocket.

Last year, his family had moved from the crumbling high-rise by the freeway to a real house, as Jack's mother called it, in the Loomis estate. It was a real house in the sense that it had two floors, three bedrooms, and a small rectangle of lawn at the back where you could sunbathe in privacy through the humid summer months. There was a community watch in the area, since many families here were affluent, and cops were scarce, and the shiny Toyotas and Volvos parked up and down these streets were natural prey for any hoods straying over from Riverside. The fact that many of the vehicles were primed with high-decibel voice alarms and some carried low-voltage electricity charges seemed to do little to deter the hoods.

People hardly ventured out anyway. Home was where the heart was, they said. The Volvos got them to work and back every day, otherwise they just sat there like museum pieces. For infotainment you stayed in, so the streets at night were almost always deserted, and tonight was no exception. Working his way up through the estate toward home, Jack felt somehow jumpy; spied upon. He sensed window blinds separating and dark, critical eyes peering out as he passed. An alarm went off in a street not far away, making him feel briefly, inexplicably guilty. A few seconds later a motorcycle engine revved.

Home was 34 Loomis Rise, where the lights were all on, upstairs and down, when Jack arrived. He saw Sandy first as he stepped inside. Half-dressed in a huge, loose, white collarless shirt that hung down to her brown knees, she passed up and down the hall from the kitchen, whispering into her cordless phone. Her latest boyfriend was Dan Morrisey, a games programmer whom Jack desperately wanted to know. Dan, he hoped, would be a great source of free software, but Jack still hadn't managed to break the ice with him. They had spoken on the phone several times exchanging high-tech gossip, but they still hadn't met. Usually Dan arrived at the house in a black BMW, swept Sandy away for the evening and dropped her off later, but never came in. Sandy never encouraged him to meet the family, Jack reckoned because she wanted to keep him all to herself. Perhaps she was even embarrassed by them.

Now, setting eyes on Jack, she retreated inside the kitchen, edging the door shut with one bare foot. He wanted to follow her in, not to eavesdrop but to raid the fridge and make coffee. He'd wait a few minutes until she'd finished. Instead he turned to his right, into the living room, where his folks were perched in front of the TV watching a documentary or news report.

"Jack." His mother winked, patted the empty cushion on the sofa beside her. "Long time no see."

"Ha ha." Jack flopped down, watching the screen. "What's this?"

They were silent for a moment until the reporter finished interviewing a fortyish woman who had just broken down in tears. Then his father said, "Seems there's been a rash of disappearances—youngsters, all about your age, all within the last two weeks or so. Some have gone missing right here, some in Germany, some in the U.S. The investigators are convinced there's a link of some kind."

"That's odd. Did they mention any names?"

"No, they're still trying to map out all the connections between them."

The report ended while he was talking; now a newscaster was introducing an item on the latest advances in prosthetic limbs. "That won't be the last we'll hear of it, you can bet," Jack's mother said.

"How can they be so sure there's a link?" Jack wondered. "Kids disappear every day, don't they, without explanation?"

"There's usually an explanation," his father said. "Scratch the surface and you'll find there are problems at home—their parents have split or are fighting, or they've fallen into bad company, or are slacking at school. You can piece together a reason in most cases. These kids, though, and there's eight of them, seem to be from well-balanced,

22

settled homes. Besides which, two of them in the U.S. are close friends."

"Maybe there was something going on that the parents didn't know about. If I had problems, how would you know unless I told you?"

"We'd know," his mother said calmly. She was giving him a look that vaguely bothered him, as if she knew he had nothing to tell. "We'd see it coming, because we care. We'd see it and deal with it, if we could."

Jack smirked. "That's a load off my mind."

"You don't have anything to tell us?" she asked.

"Of course not."

"Well, there you go, then."

She sounded pleased with herself: everything was under control. And it was true, he had nothing worth worrying her with. He couldn't see the point in confessing his fears; ridiculous, deep-down fears that one day all this home comfort would slip away and he'd wake up on some dark side street in the Riverside quarter; he couldn't tell her about the dizziness he sometimes felt after battling the Agents of Darkness on the outer continents, or the dream he once had of being stranded there. He couldn't tell her about the school tests he'd nearly failed two weeks ago because he hadn't been able to concentrate on the papers: his mind kept flitting away, out of control, to other lands, other solar systems. These weren't really problems, anyway, just things in his head. It was impossible to talk about the things in his head when he really didn't understand them himself.

23

"I'm done," Sandy said, popping her face round the living room door. "Were you waiting for the phone?"

"The kitchen." Jack followed her out to the stairs, where she turned to go up. She looked flushed and happy. "Is he coming tonight?" he asked, meaning Dan.

"Tomorrow morning. We're going to the country. He's going to show me the great outdoors. I haven't been there in years."

"He must be crazy about you."

"He is."

"So when do I meet him?"

But she'd already hurried upstairs, out of earshot.

From the fridge Jack took a bowl of leftover salad, a hunk of fresh grain bread, and a tub of lychees in coconut milk, which he ate standing up while waiting for the coffee. When he glanced inside the living room again, his folks had switched channels and were shopping for bathroom accessories. He hurried upstairs, past Sandy's room and the faint sound of synthetic music, then ducked inside his own room and closed the door.

They know where I am, he thought. *Now they can forget me, and I can forget them.*

He put the coffee cup on his desk and drew the DAT tape from his pocket while the computer booted up. It was an outmoded third-generation PowerPC, but it ran like the wind. It came with thirty-two megabytes of RAM and a two gigabyte drive, and his father had traded a nearly new set of golf clubs for it two years ago. A fair swap, Jack reckoned. In any case, if you wanted to play golf now—the nearest course was eighty miles north—you could do it without clubs. You slipped on the visor and played it virtually.

It took a matter of seconds to install the new game on the drive. Seeing its icon on the screen, it was hard to believe how much fuss had been kicked up over Sphere. It was only another item of software. The icon was a single dark eye tinted red. He sat there, staring at it.

The icon eye stared back.

No, you're not like Kyle, he told himself firmly. *You don't need this; you're not hooked before you start. No way.*

Jack North began playing the game.

CHAPTER FOUR

The first thing that struck him was the quality of light; the purple, red, and amber horizon, the blinding setting sun. The ray-traced graphics were the best he'd ever seen—he was staring into the depths of a 17-inch color monitor but he might as well have been wearing the VR visor. It was that real.

Welcome to Silicon Sphere, he thought.

Suddenly, he wasn't in the room anymore; he was standing in a deserted, dust-blown main street. The dust was a rusty, sun-baked red. Bails of tumbleweed wafted right to left in front of him, tossed by a breeze he could almost feel. White, square, two-story buildings like crumbling Spanish villas lined the street, stretching into the distance as far as the eye could see. The front of one had had its windows boarded up and painted over: the whole wall was now a huge painted mural of a Coca-Cola bottle, the red so harsh it dazzled his eyes. Ahead, Jack saw street signs and crossroads, as straight as those on a grid. He took three steps forward, and the whisper of dust underfoot made him start. When he clicked the mouse, turned, looked around, he saw a fresh trail of footprints in the dust where he'd walked.

They were the only footprints on the street.

He was all alone here in Ghost Town.

There were no clues, no game rules, so he would have to feel his way slowly. For now, he decided just to keep moving in a straight line. There were doors to open, houses to enter, but he'd leave the exploring until later, when he'd had time to soak everything in. Further along to the right, another housefront mural drew his eye. It was the face of a girl wearing Ray•Ban sunglasses. Her hair was white-blond, her lips as red as the Coke bottle's label. She didn't seem to be advertising anything except herself. Then, moving closer, he gradually recognized her: Marilyn Monroe. She wasn't a painted mural either; she was moving, turning her face slightly toward him. She was opening her lips to kiss or speak.

Jack felt his breath seize.

"Oop-oop-e-doo," Marilyn cooed.

He wanted to laugh, more from nerves than amusement. His hand on the mouse felt clammy and hot. He was waiting to see what Marilyn did next, but when she turned her face away, repeating the same slow movement as before, he realized exactly what she was: a looped morph image.

"Oop-oop-e-doo," she said.

She wasn't so hot on conversation, this girl. He wasn't going to learn much from her. He double-clicked on Marilyn's face, in case she was hiding a secret, but it didn't seem to make any difference.

Just as he began moving away from her, Jack thought he smelled perfume in the air. That was impossible, no matter how authentic the game was. Sometimes, after prolonged exposure to VR, you did feel heat or sense movement the eye couldn't see, but he'd never *smelled* anything inside the games worlds before. It must be his other senses combining to play tricks, firing his imagination. Either that or Sandy had recently split her makeup bag in the bathroom.

He continued ahead up the street. There was a distant rumble of thunder, and the wind seemed to stiffen, whipping a tuft of dead grass past his left shoulder, far above his head, then out of sight over the rooftops.

He stopped to look left and then right at a crossroads. To his left, another straight, endless aisle of white villas, and more full-color electric murals that he couldn't see clearly from a distance. But to his right, on a street named Pablo One, a shape the size of a car had formed itself out of the dust. It might be nothing more than a flourish of decoration, like Marilyn. On the other hand, if the shape was a clue, it could lead him deeper into the game. All that kept him from rushing toward it was the thought that it might not be a gateway but a trap: a snarling, digital dust monster which might gobble him up, lock him out, or crash the computer.

It was a risk worth taking, he decided. It wasn't as though he'd traveled far enough to regret having to start over; he'd quickly retrace his steps. Jack moved closer, squinting as the wind swept clouds of red dust from the street. He had a sudden, mad urge to cover his mouth to avoid swallowing; he was holding his breath anyway.

Nearer, he realized his first impression of the shape hadn't been wide of the mark. It wasn't just car-shaped; it was a bottle-green Chevrolet, probably late 1950s. Dust whipped into his face from the vehicle's windshield and body. Half closing his eyes, he began circling the car very slowly, but there was no sign of anyone inside.

Okay, okay. This must be a clue to something . . . but what? There's a mystery here . . . but what mystery?

Jack stopped, pondering the Chevy. From somewhere he imagined he heard voices—a massed choir of whisperers, all speaking at once—though this was most likely the wind between buildings. On a whim, he clicked on the Chevy's door. It flew open at once.

He was supposed to be inside it. The vehicle was supposed to transport him around Silicon Sphere. Why else would it be here? When he clicked on the seat behind the steering wheel, Jack found himself suddenly seated there, viewing the dust storm through grainy, smeared glass.

Would it go, though? There was only one way to find out. He had never driven a car before, but he knew about flight simulators, and he'd conquered the outer continents often enough. The law prohibited anyone from driving for twenty-four hours after a thirty or forty minute VR session, but he doubted that kept you from driving *in* VR.

The key was already in the ignition, waiting. A handful of other keys, smaller and larger, dangled from it, along with a key ring shaped like a minute hourglass. *Here goes,* Jack thought. He was on the verge of double-clicking the ignition when something outside the car caught his eye.

It could have been movement—dust rising and falling from the gutter in front of the Chevy—but it wasn't. What he'd seen on the pavement was a pattern of small, blurred shapes which the dust was trying desperately to cover.

If he'd started the Chevy, if he'd driven away, he would never have noticed this. But he knew from experience how crafty games programmers were. The Chevy might be here to transport him, but was it also here to distract him, to keep him from discovering something far more important?

In a matter of seconds Jack was outside on the street again. The shapes on the pavement were still there but fading fast as dust lifted, gusted, clouded the air around him like damp woodsmoke. He stared at the ground long and hard, blinking in confusion.

Footprints.

They were footprints all right, but they weren't his own. They approached from the far end of the street, the end of the street he hadn't explored yet; stopped when they reached the car, then headed back the way they had come.

The Chevy could wait. If he didn't act right away, the prints would be gone forever. The best course would be to follow the trail, see where it led, and return for the car later on. He set off in pursuit.

Now he was sweating all over. He broke off, briefly, to wipe his hot hands on his jeans. His eyes never left the screen. He didn't dare look away, for the footprints were fading further by the second. They hurried three blocks straight ahead, then turned left, along another white street, past a drugstore, past a dark basement bar with blue neon lights in its window, before reaching a sudden dead stop at the doorway to one of the houses.

Whoever he'd been trailing must have stepped in here. Jack didn't follow suit straightaway, though. It could still be a trap. When he edged closer, studying the building in detail, he saw a small sign in the window with the single word VACANCIES printed across it. A hotel or B&B of some sort, then.

Fine. So far so good . . . but what next?

He figured he had three clear choices:

Enter the hotel, take the risk.

Wait until he'd explored further. Go back for the Chevy.

Save the game, and re-enter it later at the same point, when he'd had a chance to think this through. Only a wimp would do this.

He took the risk. When he clicked on the door, it drifted open slowly, so slowly he half expected something to launch itself at him out of the dark. But as far as he could tell the place was empty; there was no sign of life here at all.

The hotel felt old, long forgotten, trapped in time. Bare plaster walls and a tiled marble floor provided a clean, cool atmosphere, but dust from the street had crept inside, too. Everything had a faintly red cast. There was a small reception desk, straight ahead, and a couple of plush chaise longues, one with a glass-topped coffee table loaded with magazines drawn alongside it. A few sagging rubber plants stood in corners. Another half blocked the front of a staircase to the left of the desk. What really struck him was how spacious and airy the foyer was, given how squat the building appeared from outside.

Jack made a beeline for the reception desk, where a guest book lay open at today's date. No one had signed in, it seemed. There was a brass bell on the counter to his right, its sheen long gone, the metal a grubby, antique brown. Well, if there was anyone on duty, they ought to come running when they heard this. He double-clicked to pick up the bell, but the sound that followed, a sound that scored through his mind like a dentist's drill, wasn't what he expected at all.

Jack North lay flat out on his bed, exhausted, still half lost in sleep. A few feet away, his digital alarm clock blared at full volume, the way he always set it on weekdays to make sure he didn't miss school. In slow motion, as the room came into focus around him—the pale, eggshell-paint walls, the old *Star Trek TNG* posters above his desk, the computer's dimmed monitor—he groped across to shut off the noise.

Jack blinked at the clock through eyes that felt gritty and raw. SAT 08:15, the LED said, but how could that be possible? It couldn't be that long since he'd started the game—five or ten minutes ago, easily, but twelve hours? You had to be kidding.

Okay, he thought. *Just pull yourself together now. There must be a simple explanation. There always is. You dreamed it, that's all. Somewhere along the line you fell asleep, and dreamed you were still in Silicon Sphere, which is why—*

Which was why it was all so fresh in his mind, as if he'd stepped inside the foyer just seconds ago. Across the room, the Mac's monitor showed its usual desktop: files and folders, not the virtual world he'd expected to see.

Sure. Fine. All well and good, except he didn't actually remember growing weary, so weary he'd been forced to save the game, quit, and haul himself the ten feet or so to his bed. He didn't remember any of that, certainly not as clearly as he remembered the foyer, the guest book, the bell. Then again, sometimes VR overload did cause disorientation for several hours. Though your body was back in the real world, your mind stayed at warp. "Suspended reality," Kyle had once called it: a kind of mild post-hypnotic trance. Well, this certainly felt like one.

He needed time to adjust, that was all. He'd take a leisurely breakfast, a walk in the fresh air, and the gap—the twelve hour blank in his head—would explain itself, slowly fill itself in. Then he'd return to the game.

It wasn't until he scrambled to his feet again, at first a little unsteadily, that Jack became aware of the mess he'd made, or somebody else had made, of the bedroom carpet. In the space between the bed and the base of his swivel chair there were five or six smudged red-brown patches. It looked, he thought, like fine sand, except he hadn't been near a beach in years. There was more of the stuff on his clothing and hands, and on the twisted mass of sheets on his bed. Jack stared, mesmerized, at the grains lodged under his fingernails.

No, this couldn't be sand. Couldn't be. He'd known well enough at first glance; he just didn't want to have to admit to himself that the marks on his carpet were footprints.

Chapter Five

On the phone, Kyle sounded even more wasted than Jack felt.

"Run that by me again," he managed to say through a yawn. "You found *what* in your room?"

"Sand," Jack said, feeling foolish in the silence that followed. "On the floor, on the bed, everywhere."

"Time you cleaned up your act then, ha ha. Why not use a vac, Jack?"

"Knew I could count on you for sound advice." Jack scowled and leaned back in his breakfast bar seat, a still untouched cup of coffee before him. "Didn't you experience any aftereffects?"

"Only the God-awful headache I got up with, but that's probably due to your phone call waking me. That and the odd sort of time-shift you mentioned. Yeah, I did spend hours doing something that only seemed to take a few minutes. It's as if there're different rules about time in the Sphere. The opposite of, say, Dark Domain, where everything flashes past at light speed."

"But at this rate it could take months to get through it. I've lost one whole night and gone practically nowhere."

"Persevere," Kyle said as if he knew something Jack didn't. "It's worth it."

"How far have you gone?"

"Can't tell you that. Can't give you any hints and I don't want any from you." He sounded adamant. "Otherwise, why play a game that offers no clues, no help? The whole point is that you know nothing. You have to find out for yourself."

They signed off, and Jack put the cellphone on the table and returned to his coffee, which was cold. He didn't feel much like drinking it anyway. He didn't have much of an appetite today. For a while he sat gazing at the formica tabletop until Sandy breezed in looking fresh-faced and full of life, which only made him feel worse. She was towelling her hair from the shower, and wore a white silk robe with navy-blue embroidered initials.

"You're up early," she said, transferring juice, cereal, milk to the table, then sliding into the bar alongside him. "If you want my honest opinion, you should have stayed in bed. You look like hell."

"When I want your honest opinion I'll let you know," Jack grumbled.

"Ouch. Did I catch you in a foul mood or what?" She splashed juice into a tumbler for herself. "Is everything all right, kiddo?"

"Don't call me kiddo. Everything's fine."

"You had a rough night, then."

"Suppose so. I don't recall. I was at the computer for a while."

"Playing games again? Personally, I'm not too stuck on that virtual reality stuff. I tried it once or twice a few years back and it made me hallucinate."

"Really!" Jack looked at her with sudden new interest. "What did you see?"

"Hard to describe exactly. It's a long time ago anyway. I suppose, when I went outdoors afterward, it was as though Newton seemed, well, unfamiliar somehow: the buildings looked less real, as if they'd been newly painted—no, as if they'd been computer generated. I seem to remember . . ." She paused, forming the picture again in her mind. "Yes, that's right. I even remember staring at the building where we used to live from across the street and thinking, 'Hey that doesn't seem like such a bad place to be after all.' Can you imagine that? It was purgatory there. Anyway, it didn't last long, the feeling. It faded a few hours later."

"You didn't like the fact that it made things seem better?"

"No. Because things weren't any better, not really. And I didn't like feeling so low after I saw everything clearly again."

"Sounds like a drug warp," Jack observed.

"That's exactly what it was. The game's a drug. But everyone's hooked on something: maybe they need to be. I mean, look at the way Mum and Dad sit studying the on-line shopping night after night. I just didn't want to get hooked on VR, that's all."

"Which must be disappointing for Dan."

"How so?"

"It's his livelihood, isn't it? And he can't sell you anything."

"He doesn't need to." She smiled.

"I don't suppose I'll get to meet him today?"

"We'll be gone a long time." Her eyes were fixed on her tumbler of juice, which she was rolling gently between her palms. "One of these days, though, okay?"

"When the spell has worn off."

"It's no spell." Sandy sounded defensive. "He's a very busy man, when he's not seeing me."

Jack pushed his coffee away and wriggled from the bar to his feet. "Would you give him a message then? Ask if he knows about Silicon Sphere." She regarded him blankly. "It's a game. He should have heard of it. Just ask him."

He didn't take the walk outdoors he'd promised himself, but instead stood outside for a time, watching the first stirrings on Loomis Rise: a small group of kids playing tag between parked cars; two women making small talk on a street corner. People were less guarded by day, it seemed. Rarely did you see anyone killing time outside after dark.

In the morning sunlight, the houses across the street looked to Jack as they always did: plain and dreary, modern and square. They didn't bear the slightest resemblance to ray-traced computer graphics, so he couldn't be hallucinating, not in the way Sandy had described. Still, his mind felt overloaded and slow, but in every other respect all was fine. In every other respect except one: he still had no explanation for the sand on his carpet.

It was still there when he returned to his room. He could try to ignore it, but he knew well enough it would not go away. The bed looked as though some small, scruffy dog had trampled over it. He removed the sheets, shook loose sand to the floor, then fetched the vacuum cleaner from the closet downstairs. By the time he'd finished cleaning the room, his head was clearing, and it was hard to see where the dirt had been. In the bathroom, he checked his reflection in the mirror, groaned at the bloodshot eyes staring back at him, the disheveled spiky state of his dark blond hair. Then he stood beneath a roaring shower and scrubbed the last grit from his fingernails; after that he was ready for virtual action again.

It didn't take long to get back to where he'd left off. Outside the hotel, the light was fading fast, the angry clouds glowing crimson and black. For the first time, Jack thought he heard music: a slow jazz ballad, so hazy and distant it seemed trapped underwater, but he couldn't be sure it came from inside the hotel. It could be outside on the street, perhaps in a café or bar. He'd investigate later.

No one came when he rang the bell, which now sounded less like a digital scream, more like a school bell in an old black-and-white movie. He waited awhile longer, but no one turned up. Finally he clicked on the stairs and began moving toward them.

How long was this taking? Seconds or hours? He had no way of knowing: the alarm clock was only a few feet away at his bedside, but he couldn't drag his eyes from the screen. In any case, time no longer mattered. He was adrift inside a mystery, and the mystery was all. The stairs were marble tiled, like the lobby's floor. An echo of footsteps, very authentic, bounced off the walls as he started up. At the top of the flight—the first and only flight, by the look of it—he rounded a corner to find himself facing a long, dim corridor with four doors on either side, each solidly closed.

This was classic interactive territory. One way or another he'd been here before; never in a world so real, so believable, but at least he knew the score from here on. Eight rooms. Eight choices. Eight mysteries. Every option represented a risk, but if you took the risk, made the right choice, there were rewards. On the other hand, choose wrongly—the room with the psycho inside it, the room with the bottomless floor—and you were back at the beginning again.

It seemed logical to try the first door he came to, but years of game playing had made Jack superstitious. Instead he clicked on the third on the left. The door opened in mechanical silence.

No psychos here, thank God. The room was empty and still, but it must have been occupied recently, because the TV was on, and there were crumpled Milky Way wrappers in an ashtray on the nightstand next to the bed. The bed itself was freshly made, with clean, white cotton sheets and a blue plaid throw. Just beyond, fine white muslin flapped at the open window, through which Jack had a clear view of the street below, where the dust storm seemed to be calming. There was a tall whitewashed wardrobe against the far wall and a matching chest of drawers, all of which opened when he clicked on them. All were empty.

Jack now turned his attention to the TV, which hissed with white noise as if someone had yanked out the cable. By clicking on the screen, Jack found he was able to change channels, skipping from a news report to a music video to an ancient Hollywood movie where dancers were dressed as bananas and pineapples.

He was on the verge of leaving the room when a door slammed somewhere outside, in the corridor. Jack froze, his right hand a rigid claw on the mouse. From here, half a dozen paces inside the room, he could make out very little through the doorway—barely three feet or so of wall and tiled floor. There were footsteps now, heavy, hurried footsteps, and a harsh sound of breathing, and then, as he looked, a sudden blur of motion as someone raced past the threshold toward the stairs.

This was the stranger he'd been tracking, for sure. Well, he, she, or it wouldn't escape so easily this time. His adrenaline pumping, Jack clicked on the open doorway, the top of the stairs and the lobby below in quick succession. The ground floor rushed up so fast he seemed to be falling, in danger of losing his balance. By the time he'd gathered his senses, he was alone in the lobby again and the footsteps were gone.

The stranger was nowhere in sight. Why the commotion, though? What had he been running from? *Surely,* Jack thought, *not from me. He couldn't even know I exist, let alone that I followed him here.*

Then maybe he'd fled from whatever had been in the room upstairs—from something he'd seen or discovered there, or worse, from something he'd done.

Whoever he is, Jack thought with a shudder, *he knows something about this place. He knows its secret. He must know its secret, and its secret must be dark, because the sound he made running past just now, that breathless gasp . . . well, that wasn't a million miles away from the sound of panic, was it?*

Jack returned to the reception desk. It was starting to feel familiar; a point he kept setting out from and returning to, never the wiser. Again he cast a long weary gaze over the lobby's plants, chaise longues and coffee table, the guest book and bell on the counter.

Clues? Hints?

The guest book.

He stopped, seeing the book as if for the first time. Until now it hadn't occurred to him to look closer. Sure, no one had signed in today, but how about yesterday or the day before that? How about the week before last?

Like everything else in Silicon Sphere, the book proved to

42

be interactive. By clicking and dragging the mouse, he was able to maneuver it closer across the counter. Then, by clicking on the top left or right corner of the page, he was able to turn back and forth through the log. Each page represented one day, which seemed to Jack overgenerous since the hotel must be empty most of the time. In any case, he was in luck. No one had signed in today, but halfway down yesterday's page was a signature, the handwriting so small and spidery it was hard to decipher. Jack looked closer, squinting. He really needed a new monitor, one with better graphics resolution. Even so, the name on the page made sudden, perfect sense to him. It was a name he recognized, and as he read it again a cold tremor passed through him like a whisper from beyond.

Greg Sharp.

Roy's contact at Northwestern, the one who'd seemingly vanished overnight from the Internet, was here? Jack remembered the mail log only too well: User unknown. Which was hardly the truth anymore. Greg Sharp was most definitely known, because he was here, right here in the virtual world.

CHAPTER SIX

The next time Jack heard his alarm, it was Monday. Riding the bus to school in East Newton, he still felt dazed and thick-headed, not yet in sync with the world. Perhaps that was why the faces of the other passengers appeared so pale and characterless, as if they'd been digitally processed. They chatted among themselves, all at once, in a language he hardly recognized, in voices which echoed around him like shouts in a vast empty hall.

The temperature had fallen over the weekend. Outside, a light wind ruffled the coats and scarves of pedestrians as they crammed the pavements en route to work. When the bus reached the Woolworth's stop on Niven Street, Jack leaned forward to watch the doors, expecting to see Kyle jump on, eager to quiz him about the game. No doubt Kyle had delved deeper into Sphere than anyone, but did he know about Greg Sharp? Jack had tried to call him at some point yesterday—the day had been such a blur he couldn't recall exactly when—but there had been no reply, and there was no sign of Kyle here at the bus stop either. Perhaps he'd taken an earlier bus; but it seemed more likely he was late.

At the next stop, a girl he knew from his programming class, Kate Kreuger, got on and found an empty seat just in front of him, turning to smile at Jack as she sat, which only made him glance down at his knees, embarrassed. She couldn't know how she affected him, so why not just return her smile, acknowledge her? He studied the back of her head, the curls of light blond hair at her blue gingham collar, while his hands bunched into frustrated fists.

There was something about Kate Kreuger. Whatever it was—and it was hard to pin down, since she wasn't exactly classically beautiful, not in the way girls were on billboards and magazine covers, what with her too-narrow face and neutral gray eyes—it caused something to shift in his gut when she spoke to him. It made him a gibbering wreck—him, the hyperspace wizard, the nerveless conqueror! It turned his legs to jelly, and one of these days she was going to notice. When the time came, he knew, he would be oh-so-cool and collected with her. He'd rehearsed the whole thing many times. Not yet, though, because life was too busy, too full. He still had to unravel the mystery of Silicon Sphere. But soon, very soon.

She turned to smile and he felt his lips seize in a dead man's rictus.

God dammit!

He watched the back of her head for the rest of the journey.

Further along, past the bombed-out Riverside buildings, the bus passed into East Newton. The area was more than a little rundown, its pale houses grubby and graffitied, its handful of shops blighted by cracked paint and illegible signs. At every turn you could see where the Riverside hoods had left their mark. Soon, Jack reflected, they would rule the roost here too. There were rumors that the school would be relocated next year.

On one street corner the husk of a burned-out car leaned against a bent back lamppost. A faint smell of gasoline hung in the air. At the next junction, the entire side of an end house had been newly painted in bright poster colors. Jack caught sight of it as the bus swung around toward the overpass, then turned in his seat for a clearer view. What he saw took his breath away.

It was a Coke bottle mural—at first he imagined it was *the* Coke bottle mural, exactly as he remembered it from the game. It wasn't. Still, since when had anything in this part of town been newly painted? If Marilyn had turned her face toward him at the next junction, he wouldn't have been so much surprised as staggered, but she didn't.

As the bus veered under the overpass with its quagmire of overloaded, intertwined lanes, Jack caught sight of Roy McKee walking the short distance from his home to the school. He was sauntering along the grass verge on the bus route, but didn't notice when Jack pressed his face to the window to try to grab his attention. In fact Roy looked lost in a dream; there was something slightly nerdish about him, with his prescription glasses, his awkward, gooselike way of moving, his backpack of books thumping and rolling about his shoulder.

Jack decided to wait for him. He hit the stop signal at the next stop and scrambled off. Just before the bus pulled out, he couldn't resist checking to see if Kate was aware of him—meeting her gaze through the glass seemed easier somehow—but she was looking the other way, deep in conversation with the woman next to her, as the bus shrank away down the road.

Seconds later, Roy came ambling up to the stop. Still lost in thought, he didn't seem to know Jack was there until the very last minute. He jumped when Jack spoke.

"Take your time. We're only five minutes late."

"That so?" Roy said. The news didn't make much impression. "Hell, but no wonder. You should've seen me half an hour ago. Couldn't get my carcass off the bed."

"Are you sick or something?"

"Just shattered. I've been getting these headaches all weekend. I guess there's some bug or other making the rounds. You can usually tell when there is; I'm always the first to catch it." Glancing back along the road where he'd come from Roy said, "Did you see the new artwork?"

"The Coke thing?"

"It wasn't there Friday, was it?"

"Not that I noticed. But now—"

"You've been playing the game, so you would notice now, wouldn't you? A couple of days of Silicon Sphere and you see a whole world of things you never saw before."

"How far into it have you gone?" Jack asked.

"Not very far. Not as far as Kyle, I'll bet. You do realize he's going to drive us completely insane over this, don't you? It's all we're going to hear from him for the next year."

"So what's new?" Moving at a snail's pace, they set off along East Newton's main street toward the school, where the bus was now emptying. "Did you check inside the hotel yet?"

"The hotel? No, but I passed it a couple of times. Is it worth it?"

"I'd say so. Last night I found a name in the guest book there. Greg Sharp's name, as it happens."

Roy looked at him, perplexed. "*Our* Greg Sharp? What does that mean?"

"That's what I'd like to know. When I first went into the game, I was sure I was alone there, everything being so silent and deserted. And then I had a sense that I wasn't alone after all—in fact more than a sense. I found footprints. And the footprints led me to the hotel, where Greg had signed in. I'm fairly certain he was there while I was. There was definitely someone else in the place."

"That's impossible. Greg was there?" Roy shook his head vigorously. "Inside the game? On your Mac? Just think about what you're saying, Jack, will you?"

"How else can I explain what I heard? What I saw?"

"Wait a minute. Just wait a minute." They were only forty or fifty yards short of the school gates, but Roy had slowed to a dead stop. He studied Jack with narrowed, critical eyes.

"What exactly did you hear and see? Tell me about it. Take your time."

"I heard footsteps while I was checking out one of the virtual rooms upstairs. Someone ran past the doorway. They were in one hell of a panic too, all breathless and gasping. And I—"

"Sound effects," Roy said quickly, dismissively. "The sounds in Sphere are very convincing, don't you agree? So you didn't actually see anyone, in the flesh, that you could talk to or touch?"

"No, but I did see Greg's name in the hotel register. He'd signed in on May 17, about the time he apparently dropped off the Net."

Roy made a face, scratched the back of his neck with four fingers. "But I swear I got an e-mail from Greg the day after that, because my reply, the one he never answered, was sent on May 18."

"So? Explanation please?"

After a moment's thought, Roy's face cleared. "Okay. I mean, I don't have an explanation for where Greg is, but I can guess why his name came to be in that book. Let's say he signed in while playing the game: he'd just got his hands on the software and he never thought to work on a copy. Then he saved the game before quitting, which meant he also saved his signature. He'd installed it inside the game. So when he ran off a copy for Bill Wallis, it was the new version, the version with Greg's signature, that got transferred.

The same version Bill uploaded to us on Friday. How does that sound?"

Very plausible, Jack thought. For once, Roy made perfect sense. It didn't explain his feeling at the time that there had been another human presence; something more than computer simulation. Sometimes, though, it was easy to forget that what you were experiencing was only simulation. That, in part, was the point of VR. He still remembered the time Kyle's cousin had loaned Kyle an all-over force-feedback bodysuit. Having worn it for a six-hour stretch the first day, Kyle had been too disoriented to stand up, let alone continue, and he'd asked Jack to try it on for size until he'd recovered.

Jack had jumped at the chance. The program installed in the suit's ROM was a meditation landscape. For five or ten minutes in real time he'd soared over hills and valleys, climbed a mountain, bathed in a clear-water stream. In so short a time he'd learned that VR at its best could allow you to feel what you'd never felt before, even if it still lacked the scents and smells to complete the illusion. And at some point, high on the mountain, he had sensed another presence, as surely as he'd sensed one inside the hotel. While perched on a ledge some distance below the cloud-capped peak, staring out across miles of breathtaking green-brown country, he felt a shift in the air, heard a rattle and whisper of wings, and knew he had company. Twisting to look over his shoulder, he saw the golden eagle which had swooped to land on a rock no more than four or five feet away from him.

Jack stared at the eagle.

The eagle stared back, oblivious. Then, with one mighty leap into the abyss, it flew.

He would never forget that moment; but he'd certainly overlooked it in Silicon Sphere. He'd found Greg Sharp's signature, heard a handful of sound samples, and arrived at the most obvious conclusion. But it was all an illusion, really it was. It was only a sim. Greg Sharp was somewhere, but it was a pretty safe bet he wasn't inside the game.

Kyle had to be somewhere, too, but he wasn't at school, and hadn't shown up by lunchtime. Monday afternoons were taken up by the Info Tech workshop, which was run by Alison Dougan, a thirtyish, New Age hippie with a wry sense of humor and cowboy boots. Kyle never missed her classes. He never missed anything which gave him free access to the Info Tech room.

Jack was adding the final touches to a presentation he'd spent the last three Mondays fine-tuning when Alison slid onto the desk beside him. She didn't say anything at first, but watched quietly while Jack worked. The presentation centered around a computer perched on a clifftop in Monument Valley, U.S.A. Basically, what he'd assembled was a simple photo montage, with just six scanned images locked together. The skies were blindingly blue; the rocks as red as the dust he'd sucked up from his bedroom floor. The twist was, the computer screen in the picture provided a gateway to anything you wanted: you could import movies or games which you then played out on the screen within a screen. You could even link into the Internet, sending and receiving messages or watching animations which other users had uploaded there.

"So where is he?" Alison asked, breaking into Jack's hypnosis.

"Huh? Who?"

"You know who. Kyle. Have you seen him?"

"Not since Friday. He's probably . . ."

"He must've come down with a bug or something," Roy called helpfully from across the class.

"A computer virus?" Alison suggested.

"That's right. He got infected by something he downloaded," another voice chipped in for good measure.

"That's bad." Alison clucked her tongue as if she'd just uncovered the truth. She plucked a floppy disk from the desktop and waved it in front of Jack's face. "The best course of action is a good anti-viral scan. He should take one of these three times a day."

"Very funny."

She put the disk down again. Floppies were still in use, though not for long, if the latest reports were anything to go by: the latest rewritable CDs were nearly as cheap now, and held six hundred times as much data. "Seriously," Alison said, "it's unusual for Kyle not to be here. Have you heard from him?"

"Not since Saturday. We spoke on the phone. He's into a hot new game, and when Kyle gets into something new he locks himself away."

"He wouldn't be doing that now, would he? Playing games when he's supposed to be studying?"

"Kyle? No. Never. He isn't like that." Jack was lying through his teeth, and she knew it.

"What's the game?" Alison said after a lull.

"Something called Silicon Sphere. Have you heard of it?"

"Are you kidding? It's the only game in town. But very addictive and very illegal." She lowered her voice to a whisper. "As a matter of fact I tried my hand at it during lunch. It's on my laptop, but don't tell anyone." She winked and tapped her nose with a forefinger, then slid off the desk again; and Jack couldn't help noticing the fine red sand fall from her boots as she strode away.

CHAPTER SEVEN

Mrs. Hallaway stood blocking her open doorway like a bouncer, her thick white arms crisscrossed on her chest. "Well, your guess is as good as mine, Jack. It isn't like Kyle to skip school. If he's ill, it's the first time I've heard of it. Just a second." Turning from the door, she called Kyle's name twice without a response. "You'd better come inside," she said finally. "If he's out, he won't be gone long. Seems to spend all the hours God sends in that room of his."

Once she'd ushered the two of them into the living room, she diverted to the kitchen to make coffee.

"Odd," Roy said the minute she'd gone. "You'd expect her to know something. And you'd expect Kyle to let *us* know something."

"Perhaps we shouldn't read too much into it," Jack said, though he was trying very hard not to. "Either he's overloaded himself and fallen into a coma or stepped out to clear his head. You know he can't leave these things alone once he's started. He has to crack the top level of every new game before anyone else. I was just surprised that he couldn't drag himself away for the workshop today."

"He's always there," Roy said. "Since when did he go AWOL during one of Alison's lessons?" Roy, who had been so composed earlier when they'd talked about Greg Sharp, now sounded rattled, his voice stiff with worry. "Should we go up and see if he's all right?"

"If he was here, his mom would know. She works from home, so she's around for most of the day."

Mrs. Hallaway came in then, nudging the door open with her knee, steadying two coffee mugs to the low, glass-topped table between the armchairs Roy and Jack were occupying. The table reminded Jack of the one in the hotel lobby in Sphere; nothing dramatic about it, just another echo of the game, like the Coke-bottle mural.

"You're welcome to take your drinks upstairs," Kyle's mom said, setting the mugs carefully on coasters. "I'm sure Kyle won't mind you waiting in his room. The pit, as I call it."

"As long as we're not intruding," Jack said.

She laughed politely. "If you were, you wouldn't be sitting there now. Goodness, we know each other well enough by now, Jack, don't we? Just don't hold me responsible for the state you'll find that room in. Kyle eats in it, sleeps in it, lives in it. Feel free to open a window if you have to. I only wish he'd pull himself together, really I do. A little self-discipline never did anyone any harm. He'll never fend for himself in the real world."

"What's that?" Roy quipped.

"I could answer that, but I wouldn't expect that son of mine to." She looked at Jack with sudden, undisguised concern. "I hope you have other things in your life besides your computer. We all need balance in our lives. Too much of a good thing can easily backfire and become a bad thing, in my opinion. Anyway . . . better step down off my soapbox before I put you to sleep. You can find your way up when you're ready."

"Thanks." Jack took to his feet in slow time, not wanting to seem too eager to escape. Mrs. Hallaway did have a tendency to lecture, although she meant well. "We'll wait five minutes, but if we miss him you could ask him to call."

"Of course."

With Roy shadowing him, Jack led the way up, turning right past the bathroom at the top of the stairs. Kyle's was the door with the laser-printed WAR ZONE—ENTER AT YOUR OWN RISK notice thumb-tacked to one of its panels.

It wasn't until he reached for the door handle that Jack had a sudden, vertiginous sense that something was wrong here. Something was not as it should be. Perhaps he'd been sleeping too little or thinking too hard, thinking of events leading up to this visit—of the footmarks in his room, the sand falling from Alison Dougan's cowboy boots, of Greg Sharp's disappearance and apparent reappearance in the virtual world—and now here he was at the door, and he didn't want to go in.

"What's the problem?" Roy asked, seeing him hesitate.

"I don't know. I just imagined . . ." Jack trailed off, wiping one moist palm on the hip of his jeans. "Jesus, I don't know what I imagined."

56

"So what's stopping you?"

"Nothing. I just felt . . ." Again, he stopped short. Fear was what he'd just felt; a quick, inexplicable rush of fear as cold and harsh as Siberian air. Fear of what, though?

Then it hit him. He was afraid of making the wrong choice; opening the door to the room with the bottomless floor or the room with the psycho inside it. Of course this was only Kyle's room, and he'd entered here many times before. But it was different somehow. The rules had changed, the goalposts had been moved. Since he'd first set foot in the Sphere, anything—literally anything—had become possible. The real world wasn't as real as it used to be.

"Oh for crying out loud, go in!" Roy said.

"Take the risk?" Jack returned. "Option A?"

"Are you losing your marbles? Go in."

Jack twisted the handle, pushed the door, and heard the sound even before he knew what it meant. Kyle's room looked at first glance as it always did: an unkempt mess, with cast-off clothing piled on the floor, tapes and diskettes and books strewn across the surfaces, a rat's maze of cables swarming between his desk and the nearest electrical outlet. On a workbench under the window there was a scrap heap of old bits and parts, dead monitors, antique CPUs from the eighties and early nineties which Kyle had determined to repair and get running again. Everything here was apparently normal, and yet, through it all, Jack heard the unmistakable sound.

"Listen," he whispered.

Roy listened.

"You hear it?"

Roy nodded.

It was the sound of the wind, whistling over rooftops and along narrow alleys; buffeting balls of tumbleweed across virtual streets, snapping unlocked doors outward and back, outward and back on whining, rasping hinges. He imagined it having set out from some far-off wilderness, crossing continents, oceans, and cities, gathering speed as it plucked up dust and grass and dead wood as it passed, sweeping tiles from roofs, bending TV antennas back on themselves. And at some point during its journey, someone, somewhere had sampled its sound, installed it in Silicon Sphere, and loaded it into cyberspace.

Kyle had left his PC switched on, and the noise seemed to be coming from there. Right now there were no pictures to match it; a screen saver threw up randomly generated fractals. When Jack crossed to the desk though, nudging Kyle's desktop mouse across its mat, the screen cleared and he saw what he'd expected to, what he'd known he would see from the minute he entered the room.

"So," Roy said, coming forward. "This is the place. This is where we start out in the Sphere, isn't it?"

Jack nodded, saying nothing. He stood there, transfixed, watching the dust whipping this way and that across the main street. Faintly, carried by the wind, there came the murmur of Marilyn's voice again: "Oop-oop-e-doo," she

sang. She turned her head slowly away. She wore sunglasses. Her lips were bright red.

"Well, where is he?" Roy wanted to know, the anxious
tone still fixed in his voice. "I'd like to believe he went out
to buy chocolate or a Pepsi or whatever. I'd like to believe
that's all he's doing, really I would."

"I'm not sure," Jack said. "I'm not sure at all."

"You knew something, didn't you? Before we even came
in here, you knew . . . Exactly what did you know, Jack?"

Jack shook his head, not lifting his eyes from the screen.
The street mesmerized him, as ever. Its mystery felt like a
small voice calling, luring him inside, where presently all
would be revealed. "I knew this was what we'd find," he
said finally. "But I don't know how or why or what it means.
Kyle is . . ."

"Kyle is what? Kyle is what?"

"He's—" Jack wanted to say it; he wanted so badly to spit
out those few foolish, simple words. It made no sense at
all—not even to him, and it certainly wouldn't to Roy—but
this was more than a crackpot hunch. This was something
he knew, that he felt in his bones. "He's in there. Inside
there somewhere," he said.

"Who's in where?" Kyle asked, behind him.

Jack jumped.

Roy gasped aloud.

The wind whistled on through the streets of the Sphere.

Kyle leaned against the door frame, rolling his jaw
around a thick ball of chewing gum. In one hand he held a

copy of this month's *Games Review,* in the other a king-sized Snickers bar. "Something wrong, boys?" he wondered, puzzled. "I step out for a few minutes and look what I come home to. How many ghosts did you see?"

"Only one," Jack said. "Where've you been?"

"Here, just here. Nowhere else." He touched two fingers to his temple. "Keep getting these lousy headaches."

"You missed Info Tech," Roy said, accusingly.

"I know and I'm sorry. I wish I'd been there, I really do. Was Alison angry?"

"More like worried," Jack said. "How come your mum didn't know you were here?"

"Probably because she'd never put her head round the door to check on me. If she'd taken the trouble—"

"You should've taken the trouble to let her know. You should've let us know, too."

"Why?"

"Because we thought . . . Never mind. It doesn't matter."

Kyle rolled his eyes heavenward as he closed the door gently behind him. He shied the magazine and Snickers bar on to the bed and sat down. "Something's got you riled, Jack. What have I done?"

"Nothing. Let's just forget it."

"You don't mean nothing, anyone can see that. Come on, give."

It was Roy who spoke first. "Jack had the idea you'd gone inside . . ." He nodded at the screen. "That you'd gone inside the game."

Kyle's face was a portrait of amused fascination. His gaze darted from Jack to Roy, then back again. "Impossible. How could I? How could anyone? Here I am. Look at me."

"Let's forget it," Jack repeated. "Anyone can make a mistake."

Kyle nodded, shifted his position on the edge of the bed. "You're reading too much into this, Jack, you must be. But that's fine; the game does that to you. Silicon Sphere really is unlike any other, isn't it? I was right all along. It's still only a game, but it does make you see the world differently."

"Never thought I'd hear that from you," Roy said. "It's only a game? Really."

"Well, it is, isn't it?"

"I'm not so sure anymore," Jack said truthfully. "Haven't you been imagining things, seeing things since you started?"

"Oh, definitely. I keep finding clues wherever I look. They're probably not clues at all, but that's the way my mind's working lately. I keep seeing stuff that belongs in the game outside the game, and I'd like to know why. I want the whole truth! I want to know what's going on in there! If there's an answer, I want it." Then Kyle became subdued and serious. "Yeah, well, don't think I don't understand what you're saying. Take a look at this, Jack, if you reckon you're the only one who's confused." For a second or two he rummaged first through one pocket, than another, until he held in his hand a bundle of sparkling, jangling chrome. He lobbed the object into the air. Jack caught it.

61

"You're kidding," Jack said, almost shouted. "This is a joke, isn't it?"

The bunch of keys felt heavy in his hand, but not quite as heavy as his thoughts. It wasn't that the keys were unique in any way; but he'd only seen a key ring like this once before, and that had been inside the game, in the Chevy's ignition. The hourglass tag was filled with red dust.

"Let me see," Roy said, making a grab for the keys. He turned them over in his hands for a moment before tossing them back to Kyle without comment.

"The problem is," Kyle said, "I can't for the life of me remember where I got them. I don't remember picking them up off the street, for instance, and I don't know anyone they belong to. So how'd they wind up in my pocket? All I know is, they couldn't have come from that Chevy. Because that's impossible. That's beyond VR, well beyond. If these keys came from there it would mean all three of us were completely insane. Well, wouldn't it?"

Jack look at Kyle Hallaway in silence. And, on the computer, the wind played on.

CHAPTER EIGHT

Afterward, Jack couldn't wait to get back to his desk and the Sphere, to see for himself if the keys were still there. If they were, then the world was a world of outrageous coincidence, but at least it would still be a sane world. If the Chevy's ignition proved to be empty, then the answer was anyone's guess.

All the way home on the bus, the same crazy idea kept leaping at him, no matter how hard he tried to push it away: Kyle had been there, he really had, whether he knew it or not, and had taken those keys from the car, regardless of how impossible that seemed. Not only that, but Mrs. Hallaway hadn't known he was home, not because she hadn't troubled to check his room but because he hadn't been home; while she was doing business on the phone, Kyle had been gone, far away, lost in VR . . .

Surely some mistake, Jack thought.

Surely such things never happened in the real world. But *was* this the real world? He was beginning to wonder.

At his stop, the bus braked and its doors hissed open, as they always did in the real world, and Jack stepped off at the intersection of Loomis Drive and Pine Street. A light wind flapped his jacket as he started uphill through the estate, but there was no sign of dust, let alone white Spanish villas or electronic murals. No, everything was fine, hunky-dory, business as usual; the houses only looked digitally air-brushed because the sun had fallen, squeezing the last of its pink frosted light through a veil of clouds. The only detail that struck him as less than real—in fact truly surreal—was the fact that Kate Kreuger was standing at the foot of his driveway when he got there.

"Jack?" she said. "That is you, isn't it? I couldn't really tell from a distance."

"Hi, Kate." He smiled the most natural smile he could muster, but she'd caught him off guard; she was the last thing he'd expected to see, and now he was speechless.

"I couldn't be sure this was your house," she said, stuffing both hands deep in her jacket pockets. "I'd been wandering around for five minutes before you turned up. People must think I'm a prowler."

"They can think what they like."

"Of course they can."

"They're very wary around here."

"I noticed. They're the same everywhere."

He nodded, and swallowed. "So what can I do for you, Kate?"

"I'm not sure. I need your advice, I think. But . . ." She shrugged, glanced up the street, down the street. "It'll take a little explaining."

He could hardly believe this was happening, but unlock-ing the front door, he led her inside along the hall, to the

bright, antiseptic kitchen. Even under the unflattering fluorescent light she looked radiant, he thought. Trying hard
not to wallow, he turned his back on her while he filled and
switched on the kettle, dragged cups from the cupboard,
spilled tea leaves across the worktop with hands that
trembled like leaves.

Kate sat in the breakfast bar, thumbing one of Sandy's
neopunk fashion magazines, occasionally glancing up to
watch what he was doing. They didn't speak for almost two
minutes, until Jack brought the drinks to the table and slid
into the bar, facing her.

"I don't know where to begin," she said quickly, as soon
as he'd settled. "I don't even know why I'm coming to you
about this, but you always seem so . . . approachable, I suppose?"

"Me?" He felt himself blushing. He was thinking of the
bus ride this morning, and how he'd avoided her eyes, answering her smile with a painful grimace.

"Yes, you. Also, I overheard what you were saying to Alison today, about that new game."

No, not the game again. After what he'd just been
through at Kyle's? "You're talking about Silicon Sphere?"

"Yes, that's it." She paused, lifted her cup from its saucer,
half raised it to her lips, set it down again. "There's something I'd like you to read," she said, unraveling a crumpled,
doubled page from her jacket. "It's a letter from a friend of
mine: a girl in Stockholm. That's in Sweden."

"I know."

"I'm sorry. Of course you do. We've been corresponding for a while, e-mailing, and this is a printout of the last one she sent. What I have to say will probably make more sense when you've read it." She pushed the page towards him across the table. "Do you mind?"

Jack shook his head no and dipped into the letter, which came from someone called Karin Mars. She'd punctuated her news with banks of exclamation marks and Smiley symbols typed with parentheses and dashes. The first paragraphs were the usual pleasantries—hello, how are you, I'm fine, and so on, but lower down the page the letter became a sudden erratic, excitable rant.

```
     I finally laid my hands on Silicon
Sphere over the weekend, Karin wrote. It's
everything people say, and if you haven't
heard of it yet, you soon will. It's hard to
describe what it does exactly, I mean how
it affects you, so it's better you discover
it for yourself. One thing I will say,
though: whenever I go there (that is, in
the game) it's like I have a hard time find-
ing my way back. Maybe it's because deep
down I don't want to come back. There's
so much more going on in there and the
real world always seems sad and empty after-
ward.
```

There was more, but Jack had already stopped reading. The letter was dated May 8, the week before Bill Wallis uploaded the software to Roy.

"It's a worldwide thing all right," Jack said, folding the letter. "I never knew it had traveled that far."

"Well, I'd never heard of this thing until Karin began raving about it. We've been in touch for—what?—nearly a year now, e-mailing each other almost every day, and this is all I've heard from her for the last two weeks. Then I overheard you and Alison in the class today, and I thought . . . well, I hoped you might be able to help."

Jack looked at her. "Help how? What's the problem?"

"Have you been following the news lately?"

"On and off."

"Have you heard about those students who've disappeared? There are a number of them, here and overseas."

Jack nodded. "There were eight, the last I heard."

"Well, it's eleven now, according to the headlines. I think Karin is the latest. They mentioned her just now on TV." She was searching his face for an answer he didn't have. "The thing is," she went on, "in Karin's letters, she used to mention some boy she knew through the Internet. They'd never actually met. It was a little like me and her, really. They were in touch, they used to send each other jokey items of mail, or bits of software, or whatever. Just over a week ago, a few days before this letter arrived, she mailed me to say he wasn't there anymore . . . on the Net. She kept getting strange mail logs every time she tried to communicate with him."

"User unknown," Jack murmured. He hardly knew he'd spoken until she saw the look in her eyes.

"That's it exactly! How did you know?"

"Let's just say it fits a familiar pattern. You can get that kind of message if you're addressing your mail wrong, but if you've been corresponding with someone for a while, that's hardly likely to happen, is it?"

Kate nodded, sipped her tea in silence.

Jack said, "So this guy . . . is he another one of the eleven?"

She took a long time before answering. "Yes." Almost a gasp.

"But what does that have to do with this?"

"Maybe nothing. It's just that this boy is the one who sent Karin the game in the first place. And I imagined . . . perhaps I'm just fishing . . . but I imagined there might be a connection."

"You're right. There might be."

"You think so?"

Which is how Jack came to tell her about Friday at Roy McKee's; about Greg Sharp's magical vanishing act, and his own trips to Silicon Sphere, of the overpowering feeling he'd had of not being alone there. He didn't tell her about the dust, or the keys Kyle had brought back from wherever he'd found them, but Kate was already sold. She listened as if in a trance, never blinking, her cool gray eyes never leaving his face.

When he'd finished she said, "And all of this happened since Friday?"

"Since I first played the game."

"Then it's more than a game, isn't it? It's as though . . . as though there's something else behind it all, luring you into playing, giving you a false sense of security, and then whammo! You disappear into it."

"But I haven't disappeared. And neither has Roy. Or Kyle." *But Kyle did,* he couldn't help thinking, *and maybe I did too without knowing. How else did those footprints wind up on my bedroom carpet? If Kyle brought a little piece of Silicon Sphere home with him, so did I: sand.*

"I know you haven't," Kate said. "But surely there's enough going on around you, Jack, to make you feel that you could. You know what I really think? I think Sphere is more than a game, and whatever it is ties all those missing persons together. We already know that at least two of them—Karin and her friend—and Greg Sharp played the game, and now nobody knows where they are. Can you think of a better explanation?"

Jack shook his head slowly, no. He was looking at Kate in fear and wonder: fear, because she might just be right; wonder, because she had finally put into words what he'd felt all along, since the first night. "Let's say you've hit the nail on the head," he said. "Let's say these students, kids, whoever they are, have been sucked inside somehow. What can we do about it? What can *I* do?"

Kate's lips smiled, though her eyes were hazy with doubt. "Well, I suppose that brings me back to why I came here," she said. "I said I wanted your help, Jack, and if it's asking too much just say the word. Really, I mean that." She paused

69

and drew a long breath. "I think we should play the game. Together. We should go into the Sphere and find out what's happening, once and for all."

He was tempted to laugh, it sounded like such a hair-brained scheme. After all, what would it achieve? And suppose, as Kyle said, it *was* only a game after all? But he didn't need to look at Kate twice to know she meant business.

CHAPTER NINE

Serious wasn't the word. Kate had absolutely, one hundred percent made up her mind. There would be no shaking her, even though she'd said the final decision was Jack's. When he asked if he might think it over, she gave him until tomorrow. There would be risks, he said, especially if Silicon Sphere really did provide a link between the missing people. "In that case," Kate said, "we'll just have to take those risks, won't we?"

She left after half an hour. Half an hour after that, he was missing her. At his desk, distracted, he stared at the red Silicon Sphere icon-eye on his computer's desktop until it fell out of focus. The virtual world was calling again, urging him to play, but something kept him from giving in. He shouldn't go in again without Kate. She'd be angry if she knew that he had. After all, the only reason she'd suggested they collaborate was that two heads were better than one; if anything went wrong they could look out for each other.

Instead, he returned to the Outer Continents to annihilate the Agents of Darkness from the comfort of his slick, customized mine cruiser. In hyperspace, territories rushed past him at blinding speed, like streaks of white lightning, as he set off for Outpost One. Enemy battleships fell from the sky like lead weights as he zapped them.

It was such easy money.

Then, on the outskirts of Zone Nine, he sensed a tremor run through his vessel, saw the view screen blank out for a second and the red LED on his console showing damage at eighty-eight percent. Not only that, but the blast had wiped out his security shields at a stroke. A lone, rickety, ill-equipped fighter had somehow drifted within range and slipped the full force of its artillery under his guard, unde-tected. Or rather, Jack had never seen it coming. There the culprit was on his radar screen, bright as a beacon, but the information had simply washed over him.

This time it was Jack's turn to spiral downward, beaten, his vessel in tatters, the ground rushing up at dizzying speed. There was a familiar flash of yellow-orange light, a black blanket of smoke, then a smirking end-of-game mes-sage:

BETTER LUCK NEXT TIME, DUDE

Damn it. This was impossible. In hyperspace, he was sup-posed to be king! He had never suffered such a crushing de-feat, never, not even the first time he'd played the game. Warzone might have been fast and furious, and sometimes downright exhausting, but never impossible as long as you kept your nerve and your concentration.

Which he hadn't. Drifting, unable to concentrate on any-thing outside the Sphere, he'd lost his edge. The more time he spent here, doing battle, or anything else for that matter, the less time he had for the virtual world. Exiting the game, he stared at the icon on his desktop again. He backed away, rolled onto his bed, still staring at the icon from a safe distance.

The icon-eye stared back. For all he knew it might even have winked at him. He wouldn't have been surprised if it had. It was the only thing on the screen that really mattered, after all. Next to Silicon Sphere, all the other software he'd acquired over the years meant nothing. It all paled into insignificance.

Play me, the game seemed to be saying.

Come on in, Jack, the water's fine. Come on in . . .

Come back to where you belong.

The knock at the door made him start as if he'd woken in shock from a bad dream. He sat bolt upright on the bed, breathing hard. "Uhh?" he called, once he'd regained his senses.

It was Sandy. She pushed the door open and stood at the threshold, peering in at him with a puzzled frown as if he'd developed a second head. "Is everything all right?" she asked.

"Of course it is. Why?"

"You're white as a sheet. You look as if . . ." She glanced quickly at the computer, then back again. "Are you sure that thing's as energy star-compliant and radiation-free as you say? Seems to me you've been getting too much of it."

"I'm fine," he lied. "Never better."

"Well, I'll reserve judgment on that. You should take a

look in the mirror, kiddo: that isn't a picture of health I see. Isn't it time you started living a little before you disappear up your own interface?"

"What do you want, Sandy?" he growled, suddenly irritable.

"Oh, yes." For a moment she seemed to have forgotten. "Just to say that I passed on your message to Dan about the game. He knew what you were talking about even if I didn't."

"And?"

"And we had a wonderful day in the country. He took me to the lakes and I got some sun." She flung out her forearms to prove the point.

"What did he say, though?" He wished she'd stop sidetracking and get to the point. "About the game?"

"Oh, that? Nothing much, actually. Except that everyone in the business knows about it, but no one seems to have any idea where it comes from, or who wrote it. Does that answer your question?"

"Hardly. Maybe I should speak to Dan."

"Mmm." She smiled. "I'll ask him to call you."

She slipped away from the door and closed it before he could say another word. Jack listened to her footsteps fading along the landing, then reclined on the bed to study the ceiling. No one knew where Silicon Sphere originated, but it couldn't have appeared out of nowhere, could it? Someone had written it, because even in this hustle-bustle high-tech world, software still hadn't figured out how to originate itself. Computers could speak and accept voice commands, answer the phone and take messages, automate almost any task they were programmed to, but they hadn't traveled quite that far yet. They still hadn't learned how to create.

He spent almost an hour checking back issues of game magazines. Three or four carried brief, mouth-watering teasers about the Sphere that he'd already read several times; one boasted a full sneak preview, spread over two pages. But nowhere did he find any mention of an author or software house. The reviewers seemed as much in the dark as the rest of them were.

The mystery deepens, Jack thought.

On the bus, next morning, Kate Kreuger saw the empty seat beside him and took it without hesitation. "God, it's windy outside," she said, breathless, shaking and slapping her navy mock leather bag. Dust scattered from it to the floor at her feet. "Even more so than yesterday. And it's bringing all this dirt with it, too. What would you say this is, Jack, sand?" She didn't give him time to reply. "There's something in the air. Can you feel it? I was standing at the bus stop just now and the sky seemed to . . . well, it was only the sun dropping behind a cloud, I suppose, but for a second or two the light changed, and everything in the street changed with it."

"How exactly?" Five minutes ago he'd noticed a sudden, brief darkening somewhere over the rooftops, but a child across the aisle had chosen that precise moment to start screaming and bellowing, drawing stares from every seat in the bus, much to its mother's embarrassment.

Kate said, "It's hard to describe what I saw exactly, except that, while it lasted, everything out there became quite unreal. The colors seemed less natural all of a sudden; people didn't look the way they're supposed to. It was almost as if they'd been—"

"Ray-traced?" Jack said.

"Ray-traced. Exactly. Computer generated. Animated." She half-smiled and shrugged. "Hell, it was probably nothing; just a storm brewing. I guess I've been thinking too hard about what we talked over last night."

"Me too."

"I didn't sleep well either."

"Nor me."

"Have you decided what you want to do?"

Jack took his time before answering, but he had only one realistic choice, and from the look in her eyes, she knew it.

"Count me in," he said finally.

Kate nodded and said, "Good. I knew you wouldn't let me down. So where do we start?"

"Easy," Jack told her, eight hours later. "Double-click on the icon that looks like an eye and we're on our way."

They were sitting at his desk: Kate in the office swivel chair, directly in front of the monitor; Jack on a creaking spare stool drawn up alongside her. Kate held the desktop mouse in her hand. She looked at him, her eyes nervous and unfocused. She laughed, but it was a laugh full of tension.

"I can't believe we're actually doing this," she murmured. "Are we demented or what? We're sitting here, about to enter some computer game—a *game,* for crying out loud!—to search for missing people. Can you imagine how that would sound to anyone else?"

"There's still time to change your mind."

"No. We agreed, didn't we?"

"Fine." His hands drummed the desk. "In that case, let's begin," he said.

She let out a gasp when the virtual main street, with its clouds of red dust, appeared on the screen. It couldn't be a million miles from what she'd witnessed this morning while she stood at the bus stop. To Jack, the digitized buildings, the brooding sky, the heavy colors were beginning to feel oddly like home away from home, he knew them so well. "Go ahead," he urged, and she clicked on a point about halfway along the main street, beyond the Coke bottle mural, flinching at the sound of their footsteps over the dust.

"Oh my God! It can't be this real, can it?"

"Look behind you," he told her. "See where we just came from."

She did, and the trail behind them was more than Jack had prepared himself for: there were now two rows of footprints in the dust, his and hers. He shook his head, marveling at the sight. "It knows," he said under his breath. "It knows there are two of us."

"How can it?"

"It can't. But it does."

Further on, she paused to admire the Marilyn morph, then followed Jack's directions along the main street and turned right at the junction of Pablo One toward where he'd first seen the battle-scarred Chevrolet. At least, this was where the Chevy had been the last time he visited; he was certain of that. But the street was empty except for a confusion of tread marks, already half covered by dust, that stretched far down the street toward the horizon.

"Incredible," Jack said.

"Huh?" Kate was squinting, as if the billowing dust troubled her eyes. "What's so incredible?"

"There was a car here before. See? Right here." He gestured at the tire marks. "Someone took it."

"Who?"

"I'd swear it was Kyle Hallaway. The last time he played, he kept the ignition keys. Somehow—don't ask me how—he brought them with him, out of the game. My guess is that he still had them when he came back again."

All the same, Kyle had his own computer, his own pirated copy of the software; without direct access to Jack's system there was no way he could leave his mark here.

"Jack?" Kate was sitting absolutely still, gazing into the screen. The wind's whistles and sighs filled the room. "There's something here . . . It's more than I expected, I guess . . . I'm just wondering, if anything goes wrong, can we still get out whenever we want?"

"I hope so." He didn't dare tell her that he couldn't actually remember quitting or choosing to quit before; that in all likelhood they would both wake up hours from now, disoriented, nursing CPU hangovers, yet hungry for more. "We can leave whenever you want. Just say the word."

"Okay. So where next?"

"Over to the left. Take us down the street to the hotel. We'll check that out before we go any further."

Entering the foyer, he had the strangest sensation of having taken another step further inside the game. The real world seemed to be fading, his own postered bedroom walls blending seamlessly into the hotel's bare plaster. Kate glanced quickly his way for reassurance, nibbling her lip as she clicked on the reception desk, transporting them to it.

"Here," Jack said. "See the register?" It was open at today's date, May 22. Again, the current page was blank. "Try going back a day or two."

"How do I do that?"

"When you click on the book's left-hand side, the pages turn backward." Still, she hesitated. "Go ahead, try it. What's wrong?"

"Nothing." But her voice told another story: taut, anxious, dry as the rasp of the page curling back when she clicked on it. "There," she said, staring in awe at the single, slanting handwritten name below yesterday's date. "Am I losing my marbles or does it say what I think it says?"

"It does, and you might be," Jack answered. "We both might be." She wasn't mistaken, but he was still at a loss to explain what she saw. Whether Kyle had signed in before or after he'd taken the Chevy was anyone's guess; but here was his signature, plain as day, and he'd even added a cryptic P.S. right after it:

Nice hotel, shame about the service. Awful slow around here, boyz. Time you got your act together . . .

Typical Kyle Hallaway, Jack thought, but how had he found his way into this interface, into this very computer? The game, he didn't need to remind himself, was nothing more than a flood of binary data trapped somewhere inside the Mac's RAM. His copy didn't exist out there in cyberspace, and hadn't since the moment Roy downloaded and transferred it to DAT; it couldn't be accessed from inside, and there was no way anyone out in the big, blue yonder could hack into it, not even by modem. Even so, it was beginning to seem that whoever played the game, wherever and whenever they did so, left their impression inside it. First Greg Sharp, now Kyle; and perhaps, somewhere nearby, eleven unfortunates recently named on the TV news.

They are here, he thought. *All of them.*

"Upstairs," he said, with new urgency. For the moment, however, Kate seemed content to linger in the lobby where the light was good and the exits were near, but he couldn't start up without her unless he took her place at his desk. There were no answers down here; but maybe, in one of the guest rooms . . .

"Upstairs," he repeated. "That's where we need to be."

"I don't know, Jack." She was sounding less enthusiastic by the minute. "There's something wrong here. It doesn't feel like a game anymore."

"It never was a game," he said, and then saw the shocked incomprehension rise in her eyes; but surely she'd known the truth before they began. Why else would she be there? "You want to know what happened to Karin, don't you?"

"Yes, but—"

"Come on, then. Or would you prefer to leave it to me?"

"I would," she said, "but I'm not sure you'd know when to stop. At least we should discuss what we're seeing. Not here, though, where it's so hard . . . to think clearly . . ."

"If we quit now, we'll learn nothing," he insisted. "We'll have to start all over again, we'll waste the precious time we've already spent, and time isn't something we have much of, not if they *are* here, which I'm pretty much certain they are." He paused. He could feel her discomfort, but it was hard to hold himself back. Outside, the wind sighed. "Remember what you said to me last night about having to take the risks? I thought you understood that."

"I do, but I didn't expect . . ." She trailed off. "I wonder whether we need help, that's all."

"I thought it was my help you needed. I thought that was enough."

Her voice sounded muted, defensive. "I thought so too."

"And now?"

She was silent for a time. Perhaps she was preoccupied

81

with the way his bedroom seemed to be slipping further away. *Here we goooo,* Jack thought. At the edge of his vision he could see the lobby's decor, its plants and draped curtains and plush furnishings. On one wall, which his large *Star Trek: DS9* poster had dominated, a hotel window now faced out to the street. Even the computer and keyboard in front of him were becoming transparent, like faint, ghostly TV images, as if the game had spilled out of the screen to swarm over the desktop. The only solid objects in sight were the bell, the guest register, and, at the point where the real and virtual worlds merged, the mouse in Kate's quivering hand.

"It's changing," she whispered. "We're really inside it, aren't we? But how? How are we supposed to quit now?"

"You'll just have to trust me," he said, meaning to reassure her, but she was looking at him as if he'd tricked her. "We'll quit as soon as we've looked upstairs, if that's what you want."

She shook her head slowly, heavily, then gave a quick nod, accepting his terms. "The first sign of trouble and we're out of here, though."

"If you say so."

"But suppose we get trapped like the others?"

"That's a bridge we'll have to cross when we come to it."

He was hardly aware of Kate clicking the mouse as the stairs approached. They ascended the stairs, bringing the hallway of doors into view. Maybe she didn't need to anymore; they were nearing that point in the game—the point you often reached in other games, too—when you simply forgot what you were doing, believed in what you were seeing, and let VR do the rest. He wasn't even aware of Kate following him to the third door along on the left, or clicking on the door to open it, but the door opened anyway, and then he was inside the room with its neatly made bed and TV riddled with white noise.

"Someone stayed here not long ago," Kate said. "Could it have been Karin, do you think?"

"Possibly. It could have been any of them."

"Hmm. It doesn't look like whoever it was left anything behind. What's over there?"

She meant on the nightstand beside the bed. On it, besides the Milky Way wrappers he remembered from last time, Jack saw two crumpled balls of paper. He was fairly sure these were new.

"Check the notepaper," he said. "Maybe someone tried to leave us a message."

Kate was unbelievably slow to react—either that, or the game was sucking up too much memory, creating a bottleneck inside the computer—because a full minute passed before anything happened. When it did, Jack let out an astonished gasp: the first paper ball lay in the palm of his hand.

"Jesus," Kate said. "How did I do that?"

I think we just crossed the line, Jack marveled. *The line between the real and the unreal. And maybe now this is where the game really takes over.* He could actually feel the paper ball in his hand.

Unraveling it, he found a handwritten memo which the author had abandoned after the first few lines. It read:

been here a week now and still cant fine alphazone. tried the mirror to get to there again but this time found only a maze of halls and streets. whole damn place is a maze. i must have done something differently the first time, like keyed in another combination. if i dont get it right this time ill be back by nightfall. dont know how much longer i . . .

"Alphazone? What kind of gobbledygook is this?" Kate asked.

"Search me. But it has to mean something; everything here is here for a reason. Try the other note."

Again, the paper ball materialized in his hand; again it took forever to do so. Definitely a bottleneck, he decided. Memory-hungry, bug-ridden applications and games had a habit of slowing the computer to a crawl; at worst, they could crash it completely, and the last thing they needed right now was a crash, because there was no telling what might happen if the game froze with Kate and himself deep inside it.

He uncrumpled the second ball of paper in a frenzy, as if his life depended on it. The same handwriting—a rushed, clumsy scrawl—began:

theres a gateway somewhere near by, think it might be in room eleven. will try again tomorrow to see where it leads. tonight im exhausted from searching. exhausted and hungry. one thing i learned: you can go a long way in virtuality, but when the food supplies run out, there is definitely a point where the hallucination stops . . .

More gobbledygook? It was easy to believe that, but rereading these words Jack felt a sudden electric charge, as if a layer had just been peeled from the mystery. The notes were either red herrings or spoilers, placed here to help the clueless dig deeper into the Sphere. Perhaps the game's programmer had planted them; or perhaps a visitor to the Sphere, Greg Sharp or Karin Mars or—

"Room eleven," he said. "Kate, get us to room eleven, quick as you can."

Kate didn't reply. She didn't respond at all. When Jack glanced up from the memo, everything in the room appeared frozen, suspended; the muslin at the windows, the white noise on the TV screen—everything had wound down to a dead stop. The bottleneck, dammit! The game was trying to crash itself to thwart him, to keep him from exploring further—and just when things were starting to move! How dare it!

"Okay," he said. "Looks like we're done here. It's a lockout. Are you ready?"

But that was when the TV snapped back to life again, snowbound screen hissing. Across the room, a gasp of wind from outside caused the curtains to flap like wings. Even so,

Kate still hadn't answered. Was she too afraid to continue or what? He turned to look at her—or rather, at where he thought she'd been standing, at the threshold of the virtual room; he would've sworn she'd been there just a moment ago. "Kate?" he said, this time in a voice that had a definite tremor. "Kate, are you there?"

But she wasn't. All he could see was the half-open door and, when he stepped beyond it, the corridor, dark, blank, and empty. There was no sign of Kate ever having been here at all.

CHAPTER TEN

She couldn't have been more than three or four paces behind him, but he'd been too steeped in the game to check on her. And now she could be anywhere; literally anywhere.

How could you let this happen? he scolded himself, furious. *You were supposed to be looking out for each other. She expected you to watch over her, for crying out loud; you could see she was afraid, that she'd sensed something coming, and what did you do? Zero. If you thought Kyle was obsessed with Silicon Sphere, what does that make you?*

He stood in the empty corridor, swaying slightly on his feet, trying to gather his thoughts. In the last few minutes the place had become as airless as a sauna, and he couldn't breathe freely, and the fact that he was close to panic didn't help. Of course, Kate could have strayed to another room; she could come flouncing back safely any minute, but he doubted it.

So what had happened exactly? He knew she'd been there at least until the first time the game bottlenecked. *And what happens,* he wondered, *after a crash? Purely rhetorical question. Unthinkable answer. If your luck's run out, and you haven't saved, the computer forgets what you were doing last; it loses its memory.* And perhaps for a time

Kate had existed in memory; she'd vanished from RAM like trashed data. Could that be how victims became trapped in the Sphere? One major bottleneck, and you were locked in?

It was an insane idea, but anything was possible here; how else could he explain being able to move around, touch objects, pick up crumpled paper balls, when logic dictated that you simply could not do that? No, of course you couldn't, but the fact of the matter was that Kate was vapor, and it was a fair bet that, if he left the game now, there'd be no sign of her in the real world either.

You got her into this mess, Jack North, now get her out.

Brilliant! Now there was an ingenious plan, but get her out how, exactly? He tried to fix in his mind the last few moments before the big freeze. He'd been reading one of the crumpled-up notes when it happened, and the note had mentioned something about room eleven; that was where Kate would be, if anywhere. He started along the virtual corridor, checking numbers until he drew to a halt three doors along on the left. Drawing a deep breath, he pushed open the door.

There was no sign of Kate, and little to distinguish the room from the first one he'd tried, except that it seemed far larger. Everything was neatly laid out, tucked and stored. The screen of a TV mounted on a wall bracket displayed a dead channel, all snow and hiss; a single small window faced out across a side street of electric murals that were playing looped ads for videophone watches, fat-free fat, newer, faster nano-chips. In contrast, the bed was a tradi-tional solid pine four-poster draped with fine white muslin. A six-foot-high wardrobe and its matching dresser were built from the same grade of pine. Aside from all this, one detail stood out in sharp relief. On the wall just inside the door was a framed map labeled "Silicon Sphere."

It had been rendered in 3D. Its streets and buildings were holograms, brimming with detail. As Jack turned his head, shadows twitched across streets, sunlight glared off metal fittings and windows. *You are here,* a flashing red LED told him, indicating a building—the hotel—slap bang in the cen-ter of town.

On closer inspection, there was more to the map than just a street plan set on a grid: the town had been laid out like a circuit board. Its houses were resistors and transistors, its thoroughfares narrow strips of solder. Jack blinked, but the illusion didn't shift. No wonder they called the town Silicon Sphere, then. The whole place was nothing but a virtual computer chip.

To the north, the grid of streets gave way to desert, or at least blank space. The handful of buildings in this area were clustered around a great dome, a dome whose name was marked as Alphazone: beyond this, the structures and streets in the Sphere had no names.

Now he turned back to the room. He wished he'd kept the spoiler notes, but he remembered well enough what they said: room eleven might contain a gateway to the game's higher levels. It could be the mirror on the dresser, perhaps. Mirrors, in myths and legends, were supposed to open all kinds of doors to other worlds. Seating himself at the dresser to check his reflection in the mirror, he understood exactly what Sandy had meant. He looked like an insomniac rabbit, white-faced, pink-eyed, burned-out on VR. But in every sense, this was only a mirror. No magic. He reached to touch the cool glass with his fingertips, but nothing happened. No help at all.

It was then that he noticed the TV remote on the dresser. It didn't occur to him that he shouldn't be able to pick it up; that he could only interact with objects in VR through a mouse or touchpad or by wearing a visor. It never crossed his mind as he collected the remote into his hands, swung around to face the TV, and switched channels, that you simply could not do this. No way.

But he could.

The first thing he saw on the screen was the girl with the giant bowl of fruit on her head. A chorus line of dancers kick stepped behind her, beaming away like three dozen whiter-than-white toothpaste ads. It was the Hollywood musical again, and it seemed to be playing in a continuous loop. Perhaps the same movie played forever on this channel, but there were no clues here, only the same old song, and Jack quickly lost patience. Next, he flicked to the news channel: scratchy black-and-white footage of guerrilla street gangs firing shots across rubbled, bombed-out streets while a soundtrack of percussion and voice samples raged in

90

the background. No, hold on, this wasn't the news channel, he realized then, but an early 1990s rap music video. When the chorus came around he skipped channels again. The breath seized in his lungs as a face appeared on the screen.

It was a guy of perhaps sixteen or eighteen, hair cropped bristle-short to his scalp, eyes hidden behind small, round-lensed sunglasses. He seemed to be trying to communicate, for he was calling to Jack—or to someone, anyone—through a fog of sparkling blue video noise and rolling horizontal bars. For a second or two the reception grew faint, then it strengthened again, clearer this time, the voice breaking through the wash of distortion.

"Help me," he said. "Help me, Jack, if you can hear—"

"Jack, did you say? How did you . . . how did you know my name?"

The boy didn't react to the question. Chances were he couldn't hear above the noise, or perhaps this was a one-way transmission, like TV before it went interactive.

"We're lost here," he said. The accent sounded American; the pale face was emotionless, thin lips slightly out of sync with the words. "Shouldn't come in here, knowing so little . . ." Static cut him short for a couple of beats. He faded out, then in again. ". . . hearing me? If you are, don't wait, Jack, don't hang around unless you're planning to stay . . . for one hell of a long time."

"Where are you?" Jack said. "Is someone keeping you prisoner here?"

Again, the boy didn't answer. His voice distorted beneath

interference as he continued: "You're not yourself anymore once you're playing this game. Have you noticed that?—how things change? You're one with the computer and the computer is God, that's the way it is. Sure, someone made the Sphere, but not in the way we'd expect. No one wrote it. No one dreamed it up. It's more than just a stream of binary code. Believe me, the damn thing's alive. From the outside everything seems so empty and deserted, but don't let that fool you; it's crawling . . ." Fade in, fade out. "There's a lifeforce here, but I'm not sure it's human . . ."

"Who are you?" Jack demanded, but in vain. "Are you Greg Sharp? And if not, where is he? Where's Kate?"

The boy didn't speak another word, or if he did, it was swallowed by static as the screen died again. Almost at once another face appeared where the boy's had been: a girl's face this time, a terrified face, screaming. "Matrix," she seemed to be saying. "Matrix . . ." He still couldn't make head or tail of it. It was as though the girl were trying to communicate in another language—French, German, Swedish.

Swedish? he thought.

Karin Mars?

"Are you her? Are you Karin?" he asked, but Karin, if it was Karin, merely raised her hands, fingertips straining upward and forward, as if to claw her way out of the screen. For an instant her eyes, bright with terror, seemed to meet his across the void. She saw him, he was certain, as clearly as

he saw her. There was contact, no question, and she was im-
ploring him to help. But how? What could he do? If he'd
been able to help Kate, he would have. If he'd known what
really went on here, he would never have let her come.
Never.

Already the girl's image was fading into the fog. He
wanted to look away, to bury his face in his hands, but he
would still see her silent, wide-mouthed scream in every bad
dream from this day forth. Seconds later she was swallowed
by video noise, and snow settled over the TV screen, and
this time the snow didn't clear. In the silence that followed,
Jack felt his heart tripping like a dull, sampled drum between his ears. The world whirled around him. He sat for a
time, clenching his hands together to keep his whole body
from trembling.

He would return to room eleven later, but now, more than
anything else, he needed to escape outside, to be somewhere else—anywhere else. Even the never-ending dust
storm seemed more inviting than the airlessness up in the
rooms. What had happened since he arrived here with Kate
had changed everything, and for the first time, he felt
afraid.

There had been a time, Jack reflected as he entered the
lobby, when the world was round, home was where the
heart was, games were games, and reality really was reality.
But whoever created this domain had thrown all those rules

out the window. Here the danger, the imminent danger, wasn't just virtual. Here, the cry of the wind was more than that: it was the call of lost souls. Above all, this world wasn't even round.

It was shaped like a circuit board.

THE HACKER'S TALE

CHAPTER ELEVEN

I was born for this, Eddie Matrix thought. *It was meant to be.* He had created this world from the ground up in less than one day—eat your heart out, God—and now the lost souls were beating a path to his door.

He had always loved making things. By the time he entered the third grade, Eddie had built his first Unix workstation, cobbling it together from the bits of computer wreckage he'd brought from far-flung junk stores and scrap heaps to his father's den. The Internet was growing, Micro$oft was a word that Dad spat out through clenched teeth, but at that time VR was a rumor, talked about in magazines, toyed with in movies, but in truth no more than a baby still learning to walk. By his seventh birthday, Eddie's parents proclaimed him a genius: he was at work on his own programming language and had lifted enough parts of the Macintosh operating system and IBM's OS/2 to start compiling his own graphical user interface, Matrix OS.

School was a pain, though. Somehow it got in the way. There, he was expected to waste precious time studying dinosaurs, reading books with pictures, adding and subtracting, while what he really wanted was to be at home belting out code in C++. At least his parents encouraged him: his father who had been fired from Micro$oft and now worked as a programmer for a small software house that specialized in electronic organizers, reckoned that Eddie would one day become president, or at least the next Bill Gates. His mother, a telephone sales officer at Dell, wasn't convinced this was a good idea, but agreed that Eddie was headed for great times.

Now, looking back, Eddie Matrix couldn't help wondering what had become of the years between then and now. He remembered the early days clearly: the long hot California summers when he'd retreated to the cool half-dark of Dad's den, where a thousand spare parts littered the workbench and most of the desk where his workstation sat. The den was in the basement, and the narrow shaft of light beaming in through the single, small, barred window just kept him in touch with the outside world as he worked. Occasionally he'd glance up from the monitor, drawn by the rise or fall of sunlight, or the sound of Bob, the dog, barking, or the fresh smell of grass as Dad mowed the lawn, but he never felt tempted to leave his post.

No, Eddie thought, *I was born for this. Born to be one with the machine.*

Just one small boy and his workstation, and the long, long hours of summer. It was all he really needed: the lure of the code, the hypnotic pull of the flickering monitor no more than twelve inches away from his eyes. At times, toward the end of a long hard day, he would absently reach out to brush the screen with his fingertips, wishing he could touch what lay beyond. There was a whole world out there, on the other side of the glass. Hooked up to the Net on a dedicated line, he could pull in live pictures from the control room at NASA, download public domain files from the CIA, or take part in video conferences with kids very much like himself. He could jump from Tokyo to Moscow to London in seconds, checking the weather, reading news, or taking virtual tours of the world's great art galleries, museums, and mansions. At night, in bed, a cursor blinked behind his closed eyes. Between his ears, his brain gave a gentle settling sound, like the crackle of a hard disk being written to.

At fifteen and sixteen, he was poised for a brilliant career. School, when he did apply his mind to it, was a breeze. He was years ahead of them all. The problem was, he never felt like he fit in. For one thing, kids his own age couldn't understand him or the things that he talked about; they weren't like people on-line. And besides pointless work, school meant sports, and he hated all sports except the interactive on-screen versions at which he did well—and the attention of girls made him nervous. Each break and lunch hour, instead of hanging out with the others, he retreated to the library's computers while the mob pouted and mingled outside. The school's PCs were nothing compared to his own, and still ran slow Stone Age software, while the light, bright, fluorescent atmosphere of the place made him long for the dark of the den.

Night after night, Eddie Matrix walked home from school alone, but he shed no tears, never wept for himself. After all, he was destined for something better and higher: he belonged not to this world but to the world of the CPU screen and what lay beyond it. His time was coming, he knew it.

One night, hooked into a video conference that spanned the globe, he fell madly in love with the image of a girl from San Francisco. Her name was Natasha Golding; she was a year or two older than Eddie. Her long, dark blond hair was braided, her smile took his breath away, she wore brightly patterned clothes that reminded him of Polaroids he'd seen of his mother, taken some years before he'd been born. The thing about Natasha was that she never made him feel awkward; beauty hadn't spoiled her, in fact she struck him as shy. In conversation she seemed fascinated by what he'd achieved so far in electronics, what he planned to do after leaving school, and she wanted to know more. Once, he uploaded a copy of his operating system, Matrix OS, to run on her PowerPC. She told him it was a brilliant invention, years ahead of its time. In return, Natasha sent him a 3D adventure game she was fond of. It turned out to be primitive, but he grew to love it because she did.

She lived with her mother, he learned. Her father had left home and moved east five years ago. Despite that, she was happy and natural whenever they chatted. She seemed eager to keep the lines open between them. This was the world beyond the screen he'd secretly dreamed of, and when his parents announced a trip to a software conference in San Francisco, Eddie jumped at the chance to go with them.

He decided not to tell Natasha; this would be her surprise. He'd drop in to see her unannounced, and if all went well, they would spend the rest of the week together: she'd show him the sights while they planned their future. In Eddie's head, this was all taking place at the speed of light. He couldn't slow himself down. In the days before leaving he grew restless and tense, unable to concentrate at school, unable even to work in the den. Although the flight lasted less than an hour, he never sat still for a moment. For the first time, he was chasing something outside the computer, something that lived and breathed in the real world.

At least that was how it seemed at the time.

Eddie Matrix looked out across Silicon Sphere. As the memory flooded back to him, the winds outside rose with a shout. A bale of dry grass wafted into the line of his vision, hung in midair for an instant, then vanished into the swirl of brown dust. Overhead, the sky's crimson bled deeper.

Storm's really building now, Matrix thought. *Storm's going to be a humdinger tonight.*

He turned from the window, his vision swimming, unfocused. Sometimes the virus just got the better of him, and at those times, his head close to bursting, he knew his only option was to give in. For a moment or two he covered his face with both hands, and felt his face hot and moist, realizing only then he'd been weeping.

■   ■   ■

When he stepped off the plane, he was a child again. Eager with excitement, he couldn't relax until his parents had checked into the hotel and started unpacking. He didn't stay to help, or even to freshen up, and when his mother asked where he was heading in such a hurry he told her he'd be back inside an hour.

It took much longer than that, not least because the cable car dropped him a quarter mile short of Natasha's address. Still, the walk, all uphill, helped to unwind him, coaxing the tension of the flight from his bones. A cool breeze cut across town from the distant bay; the summer sky was a clear, placid blue; the houses, decked out in cool pastel pinks and greens, lined the route to Natasha's like a series of Norman Rockwell paintings.

He'd memorized the address long ago, before coming to San Francisco was ever a prospect. It hardly mattered that he hadn't a clue which direction to go in, which broad leafy street to take, because his senses were sharp as a cat's; he could practically feel his way there. In the months since their correspondence began, he'd grown to know Natasha so well he could visualize the place where she lived. Even the sound of her address—7 Acacia Drive—fixed crystal clear pictures in his mind: a large, sprawling lawn overhung by green trees, an old metal-framed swing left over from childhood, the seat swaying gently in the breeze.

That was the mental image he'd had for so long; so the sight of the house—he double-checked the mailbox outside to be sure—stopped Eddie Matrix dead in his tracks.

Halfway along a street of brightly painted clapboard houses was one that looked forgotten and long overgrown. The grass hadn't been cut for some time, and the paint was flaky and dull. The windows were so filthy they might've been made of tinted glass. It was as if they'd been purposely neglected, to keep the light out.

Natasha lived here? Natasha, with her bright, broad smile and her poster-colored clothes? On the monitor she looked born for the sunlight; she couldn't possibly survive in that darkness, that place of decay.

Eddie started up the drive to the door, suddenly tense again. Now, for the first time, he had serious doubts. There was something about this scenario that didn't feel right.

All the same, he thought, *you've lived most of your life in a dark room, haven't you? Locked away down there in the den you reached out to the world and found . . . Natasha. Well, who's to say she wasn't doing exactly the same all along? Perhaps, like you, she just needed someone to let the light in . . .*

So perhaps this wasn't as bad as it seemed; instead, it could be the final proof he needed. They were soulmates, Natasha and him. They were both completely alone. In darkness, reaching out through the computer's glass eye toward some kind of contact, they had found one another. And so—

Eddie rapped the brass door knocker that was shaped like a snake's head twice and waited. In the silence that followed, a tingle of nerves fluttered the length of his spine.

Here he stood, perched on the edge of the city, surrounded by houses decked out in bright colors, their lawns as green as a pool table, and there wasn't a soul in sight. *You're supposed to feel afraid in the night, in the dark, in some shadowy inner city alley,* he thought, *not out here in broad daylight. Come on, Natasha, enough is enough, let's move this along. Answer the damn door, will you?*

He felt his breath catch in his lungs. There was movement inside the house, some short distance beyond the door. He heard somebody cough—a guttural male noise, certainly not Natasha or her mother—and then a key or bolt was being rattled. After another brief lull the door began swinging inward, and he found himself staring into the eyes of a burly, ginger-haired boy a little older than himself.

The kid, rather pudgy, his eyes heavy and dark behind thick-lensed prescription glasses, blinked at Eddie as though he'd just woken from a heavy siesta. "Yeah?" he said.

Eddie was lost for words. He could only imagine he'd misread the address after all. "Natasha? Doesn't Natasha Golding live here?"

"Who?" The kid's face misted over. "The name is Speakes, friend, not Golding. Doesn't *who* live here?"

"Her name's Natasha. Just a girl I got to know through the Net. I'm . . ." Confused, Eddie retreated slightly. "I'm sorry. My mistake."

"Wait."

He'd taken a couple of steps back along the driveway before the kid called him back. He turned and saw the kid

104

scratching the back of one ear, watching him with sudden new interest. "Well?"

"You say you met her on the Net?"

"That's right."

"What gave you the idea she was here?"

"She gave me her address. We've been in touch for a while, not that we were using snail mail or anything; we just exchanged that kind of info as a formality. I came a long way to see her today. I suppose . . ." He broke off; he didn't know what to suppose. He couldn't, didn't want to believe she'd fed him the wrong address to protect herself. Surely she knew him too well for that, well enough to trust him with personal details. "We must've gotten our wires crossed," he said weakly.

"Maybe," the kid said. "Then again, maybe not."

"Huh?"

"How exactly did you meet this girl?"

"Through a video conference. You know: cameras hooked up to computers, conferencing software. That was the first time. Later on, we . . . the conferences were more private, between her and me. Why do you ask?"

The kid was still fussing behind his ear, twiddling with the stem of his glasses. The lenses bobbed unnervingly in front of his eyes, reflecting the light on and off like Morse code. "My brother, Leon, was into that scene," he said. "He packed up and cleared out a few weeks ago though—went to Silicon Valley to seek his fortune, or hustle for a job, whatever—but he left most of his gear behind when he went. Said he didn't need it anymore. It's all still up there in his room. I was wondering . . ."

"Whether his computer was playing host to Natasha?" Eddie said quickly.

"I don't know how it all works. Leon was always the brain here, not me. I just wondered . . ."

But it felt like a real possibility. Perhaps Natasha had accessed the Net by connecting to Leon Speakes' computer, an Internet gateway, using his domain address as her own. For reasons known only to herself, she'd used his snail mail address too. "Would you mind if I looked at his computer?" Eddie asked. "If this is what I think, I could probably trace Natasha from here. It wouldn't take long."

"You're a stranger. Why should I trust you?"

"You can watch me if you like. I only want to see the computer."

The Speakes kid took a moment to chew this over, then gave a lethargic shrug. "All right. I guess it can't hurt. You seem to know what you're looking for. Five minutes, though, and that's all."

Ushering Eddie inside to the hall, he led the way up a flight of polished bare wood stairs that clattered underfoot, turned sharp left at the top, pushed a door open and inward and stood leaning against the jamb, short of breath. "Remember, five minutes," he said, moving back to the stairs. "I'm getting the flu or something and I need peace and quiet around here."

"I'll be quiet," Eddie assured him. "And quick." Waiting

until the kid had gone down again, he stepped into the room.

It was cleaner and brighter than he'd expected. Hell, compared to this, his own room at home was a dump. Here pillows and sheets on the narrow bed were fluffed up and tucked in; books and CDs formed orderly lines on their shelves; work surfaces were free of dust and clutter, with paperwork stacked in organized piles. He wasn't here to admire the housekeeping, though. There was a mystery to be solved, and quickly. The computer, perched on a sturdy pine desk beneath the window, hadn't drawn his attention at first because it was switched off, or at least the monitor was. As he moved nearer, he heard the faint whir of the internal fan, and a crackle of hard disk activity.

So Leon Speakes had left home, but he'd left the computer running. Why? *Because I was right,* Eddie thought. *Not because he forgot to power down but because what we have here is a host on the Net with people calling in and out all day long.* This was where he'd met Natasha: she'd connected here, but she hadn't been calling from here. So why the mystery? Why had she misled him by posting the wrong address?

Dropping onto the swivel chair at the desk, Eddie Matrix switched on the monitor and waited. The seventeen-inch Sony flickered and sparked to life with a fizz of static. As it did, two things struck him immediately. A copy of the operating system which he'd posted to Natasha had been installed on this computer; it was running Matrix OS. The 3D icons and gleaming chrome control pads with their brightly colored, marbled spheroid buttons were unmistakably his.

He was mystified and vaguely irritated by the discovery. He'd uploaded the software for Natasha's personal use, but somehow it had fallen into Leon Speakes' hands. How? Well, maybe Leon knew Natasha, and she'd allowed him to copy the system for himself: that seemed a logical explanation. Still, if that was the case, it felt to Eddie like a kind of betrayal. The software had been a gift to Natasha, for her eyes, her PC only. It was as though he'd sent her a love letter which she'd gone and shown to her friends.

The second thing that caught his attention was harder to figure out. At first he didn't know how to react. Several windows on the display were active but collapsed down to small icons, a design touch he'd borrowed from Micro$oft. When fully expanded, these were the windows in which you entered word processing text, or edited graphics, or viewed others in video conferences, depending on which applications you were running. Matrix OS was a multitasking environment, which basically meant you could do several or all of these things simultaneously.

Curious, he clicked on one of the icons to open it. The window zoomed out to full view, occupying the top left quarter of the screen. It contained what looked at first like a geographical relief map, a complex series of lines describing a shape. The shape seemed to be moving, slowing rotating to provide a 3D view. As he studied, Eddie began to understand that this wasn't a map of a landscape; it was something more than that, something almost too familiar. He clicked open another window, which sprang out to fill the screen's top right, then sat back in the chair, aghast.

Here was Natasha's face, the easy, smiling face he'd come to know almost as well as his own. Her lips moved conversationally, but without sound. Her chestnut-brown eyes stared blankly straight ahead, unseeing, as if her mind were totally empty. Seen like this, the smile looked as genuine as a showroom dummy's. She too was rotating inside the window so that now he saw her head on, now profile, now from behind, just like the map. *Oh Jesus,* he thought. *Just like the geographical map. Exactly . . . exactly like the map.*

Something, somewhere inside him capsized. For an instant he felt sure he would faint. It took almost a full minute before he realized why his head seemed so crowded with noise, why he felt so near to the edge of a scream. The map was just that; a physical description of Natasha; the outline from which Natasha herself had been rendered.

The beauty he'd fallen for wasn't real. She'd been graphically generated, either from scanned photographs, or straight from the map he was studying now. Either way, she was no more human than a character in some adventure game. She didn't exist, and she never had.

She? he thought. Eddie's head was still swimming. *Whaddya mean, she? The only word for what you're looking at right now is . . . It.*

He didn't need to spend any more time here. Dazed and shaken, he swung himself up from the desk and left the room without so much as a backward glance. He was halfway downstairs when he saw the Speakes kid in the hall, watching him.

"Did you find what you were looking for?"

"I . . . think so." Eddie's mouth felt so parched he could barely force out the words. "More than I was looking for, in fact."

"That's good. So you found where that girl of yours really comes from?"

"You could say that."

Eddie kept on walking, out the front door, back along the driveway to the street. It felt cooler outside than before. There were no good-byes. Behind him, the Speakes kid closed the door softly. For a while, Eddie stood by the mailbox, supporting himself against it to keep himself upright. If he let go now, he would fall. There was no air in his lungs, not a thought in his head. His mind reeled, as if a storm was whipping up somewhere inside.

Storm's going to be a bad one all right, Eddie thought, all these years later, sprawled on the couch in his office in Silicon Sphere. He wasn't even bothering to watch the storm now; he could see it all too clearly in his mind. Hell, never mind seeing it; he was orchestrating it. It came from somewhere inside him. As the pain of old memories rushed at him, a distant groan of thunder echoed across the virtual world outside. As he wept, the rain began rapping his window.

Once, he had been normal, destined for great things. The world had been his oyster then; everything seemed to be going his way. But no party lasts forever, and Natasha had been the first chink in his armor. Through her, he'd taken his first full step toward madness and the thing he'd finally become.

So he'd fallen for a rendered image, not a real person at all, and for a while he was devastated. Then, sometime in late summer the same year, it finally hit him: the machine gave him everything he needed in life. He belonged to the code, not to the world of people and nature and feelings. It was okay to love machines. Who needed people? There was no need to look any further. In time, he stopped losing sleep over Natasha. She didn't haunt his dreams anymore. The only question that still preyed on his mind was, "Why?" Why on earth had anyone dreamed her up in the first place? Why had she—it—entered his life at all if only to hurt him?

The answer was waiting on September's newsstands. In an idle moment in town one afternoon, Eddie Matrix picked up a handful of magazines, *Omni* and *Byte* and a couple of others, shelled out the twenty-five dollars and began reading the instant he found a seat on the bus home. There was one publication, *Inside Computing,* that he read each month religiously. Its in-depth news and programming articles were the best of their kind. On this issue's cover were several teaser headlines to tempt him inside: NANOTECHNOL-OGY LATEST said one. And another, THE SENSATIONAL NEW OPERAT-ING SYSTEM THAT WILL CHANGE THE WAY WE COMPUTE.

It was the second item that he turned to first. According to the contents page, the story ran for fully eight pages. That, by *Inside Computing* standards, was a major story. Eddie flipped through toward it with bated breath, thirsty for knowledge. *One of these days,* he told himself, *these hacks will set eyes on Matrix OS, and then we'll see what's cool and what isn't.*

But they'd already set eyes on Matrix OS. That much was clear from the first page of the article, which carried a full screen shot of the interface, complete with chromium control pads, floating multicolored menus, and resizable 3D icons. Eddie stared at the page in sheer disbelief. *But this is mine,* he thought, aghast. Perhaps he even gasped the words out loud, for several passengers on the bus turned in their seats to look at him. *This is my work! All my work!*

Yet according to the magazine, the all-singing all-dancing operating system had been written by someone else: Leon Speakes.

> *The twenty-year-old wizard,* the article continued, *has achieved a winning balance of features and functions. Many of these can be found elsewhere—protected memory, full multitasking, built-in Internet capabilities, proper voice recognition, drop-dead gorgeous customizable interface—but we've never before seen such features so well integrated, so easy to fathom, so lightning fast in operation. Speakes, who hails originally from San Francisco . . .*

There was more, but Eddie could hardly go on. Suddenly he understood everything; the catastrophic truth had been staring him in the face for so long he'd been blind to it. If Leon Speakes had created Natasha, he'd done so to lure un-suspecting saps like himself into divulging their great ideas. While Eddie had posted the OS as a gift to the love of his life, Speakes had been bleeding him dry. Speakes, the rot-ten pirate, had stolen the software, claiming it as his own.

It was easy to imagine the rest: Speakes runs off to Silicon Valley, demonstrating the software at computer shows, fix-ing meetings with industry leaders. And the moguls are im-pressed; mighty impressed. Suddenly PC manufacturers, checkbooks in hand, are falling over themselves to meet him. But instead of selling the operating system outright, smart Leon Speakes licenses it; within a few months, the Matrix OS will come preloaded on every new Dell, Compaq, and Panrix on the market. Speakes makes a killing, and within two years has a stranglehold on the industry.

Later, Eddie read an Internet news group called comp.sys.vanguard. This was a conference devoted to the operating system Leon Speakes had renamed Vanguard. There were several thousand articles in the group, most of them posted within the last week. Apple was worried, Micro$oft too. Before long, someone would try to buy Leon out. Meanwhile, computer nerds from around the world were panting with real excitement. Reading the group, Eddie learned two key things. First, that Speakes looked un-stoppable: if he hadn't wasted weeks mourning over

Natasha, Eddie might've had a chance to stop the thief, but now it was far too late. The pirate had it made.

Second, Speakes had established his own company office in San Diego, built atop a money mountain. According to a press release posted to the news group, Speakes already had a team of programmers working on a new, enhanced version of the software, Vanguard 2. It was reading this press release that gave Eddie Matrix the idea.

It was high time he found a job.

One week later, he took a Greyhound bus to Cupertino. A week after that, he was working for Leon Speakes.

After that, there was no looking back.

Chapter Twelve

"I don't get it." Jack North leaned forward across the half-moon counter in Paolo's coffee bar. "You haven't seen any of these people in here?"

The girl behind the counter shrugged and twitched a smile. "Sorry, no. Things might pick up later on if you stick around." She was pretty, he thought, with deep brown eyes and dark blond hair framing her pale oval face, but she didn't have much to say.

Apart from the two of them, the coffee bar stood empty in the muted light of Tiffany lamps that seemed to fade sharply as the storm closed in. Tables wore neat red check tablecloths, the wood floor was a polished but shoe-scuffed maple, a digital jukebox played sounds from the eighties and early nineties. He could almost have been back home— almost, except for the weird fact that none of this was actually real.

On entering the café, he'd been relieved to see another human face, and the smell of real coffee had steadied his nerves. This seemed as good a place as any to shelter from the storm: outside, streaks of white lightning were beginning to crisscross the sky. Rain was coming.

"Going to be a humdinger tonight," the waitress said, refilling Jack's cup with steaming hot liquid. "Storm's going to be a bad one all right."

"You can say that again."

"Storm's going to be a—"

"I didn't mean say it again," Jack said. "I just meant . . ."

The girl looked at him. There was something behind those dark eyes, something empty and cold, that unnerved him. "How long did you say you've been here?" he asked.

"In this job? As long as I can remember. Which probably isn't long at all. It's hard to keep track of the time in a place like this. The time's never what you expect it to be."

"How so?"

She showed him her wristwatch. "See that? Five-forty, Pacific time. And see *that*?" She gestured toward the digital wall clock over the bar. It read 12:33. "And if you walked about three blocks east to the town clock up on that big building there, it'd say something else again. Really weird. I've yet to see two timepieces here that were synchronized. I just wish someone could explain it to me."

Jack took a sip of his coffee, hot, black, and bitter. The caffeine felt like a fingertip prodding the front of his skull. "It could be," he said, "that the Sphere is a place without a time zone. It exists outside time."

"Huh?"

"Meaning it's a game that's played all over the globe, and no two people get lost in it and arrive here the same way or at the same time. It's like one great big desktop conference; we're not actually here, we just think that we are. See, my

116

own watch is set to three-thirty, GMT. I come from another place and time."

The waitress narrowed her eyes. "Sounds cool to me. Can't say I know what you mean, though."

"So what happened to you? You must have played Silicon Sphere."

"I can't rightly remember." She was frowning; the question had thrown her. "I just remember . . . I don't know. It seems a long time ago."

"What about your family and friends? You must remember them."

"Oh, sure. Sure I do." But she didn't sound convinced. "Sure I do."

"Is this what happens if you stay too long?" Jack wondered. "Eventually you forget where you're from—you forget everything you've left behind?"

The waitress shrugged. "Search me."

"Don't you care? Sounds to me like you're not even interested."

"This," she said, looking around the dark, empty café, "is what I know, okay? Gimme a break, will you?"

She went back to work then, clearing and stacking crockery, sweeping crumbs from the bar. Her movements were mechanical and quick, as if she didn't need to think about what she was doing. As if she'd been programmed.

The truth had been staring him in the face from the moment he walked in here. As she swept the crescent bar in front of him, Jack reached out, grabbing the girl's wrist, smothering her hand with his. The waitress flinched, tried to jerk free.

"What . . . what are you doing? Get *off* me."

"I should've seen this coming," Jack said, letting go. There was no warmth in her fingers, no pulse beat, no spark of life, only a faint static charge as she pulled her hand clear of his. "I have to hand it to you, miss, you're very real. Very convincing. You really had me going there for a while."

The waitress—not flesh and blood after all, but still a brilliant creation—backed up, nursing her wrist. "I don't know what you're talking about. You're crazy, you must be crazy, you'd better get out of here now."

"Don't you know what you are?" he asked. "Don't you know who you are?"

"I do. Of course I do."

"Then tell me your name. Just tell me your name, and I'll go."

"Natasha," she said. "I work here, I live here. This is my home. My name is Natasha. Beta release version number I.0B3. There. Are you happy now?"

"I wouldn't say happy exactly," Jack said, lowering himself from his bar stool. "I'm sorry if I upset you. I needed to know."

The waitress watched him as far as the exit, then went back to work, stacking clean crockery, wiping clean surfaces, a lifeless beauty in a grade-Z job. She didn't ask for his money when he left, even though she'd served him two coffees. Which was just as well, Jack thought. He couldn't be certain he had the right currency anyway.

Chapter Thirteen

It didn't especially faze him to learn the truth about her. This was something he had to get used to—not trusting his senses, not believing anything he saw or smelled or touched. Even the coffee he'd consumed inside hadn't left much of an aftertaste; perhaps he'd imagined that part of it, too.

Outside, though, the rain felt real enough. In the rip and rush of storm-charged air, it stung like hail. Red dust whipped across the main street, forcing Jack to fumble blind, eyes tightly shut, toward cover. He should've stayed in Paolo's coffee shop; despite having only a creepy virtual waitress for company he would at least have been safe and warm, but now he had little chance of turning back. The winds drove him on.

There were no two ways about it: he would have to start searching for Kate tomorrow. Right now his best bet was to find shelter, and wait. He thought about finding the hotel again—at least there were beds there—but how could you find anything in these conditions?

Away to his left, neon lights glowed somewhere through the thick curtain of dust. There was a sound, he thought, of someone or something weeping; a long, drawn-out, hollow wail like the flow of air trapped between buildings. Reaching the end of the street, Jack felt the wind seize him again, this time dragging him sharply to his right and around the next corner. Visibility was no better here, and he had to feel his way along the walls, palms scraping the brickwork, in an effort to move forward in a straight line.

Then, for a matter of seconds, the wind seemed to drop, and he heard the vague sound of jazz music wafting toward him. He'd heard that sound before, at the hotel, he remembered. In such a highly digitized world, the rise and fall of cool acoustic piano and saxophone notes seemed alien but somehow reassuring, a reminder of things he'd left behind—his father's music library with its hundreds of obsolete vinyl records; the soundtracks of old movies featuring gangsters, pool halls, racketeers. He couldn't make out the melody, couldn't quite fit the notes together in his mind, yet the music sounded more immediate and live than any recording. It was coming from somewhere across the street to his extreme left, perhaps from a bar where people would be gathered together. Real people? Turning back into the wind, he forced a path toward the source of the sound.

He heard the sign creaking outside the club's entrance before he could distinguish it through the dust. Crossing the street to the far pavement, he was almost at the steps leading down to some darkened basement when the wooden board swinging back and forth in the wind above them fell into focus. There was no name on the sign; just a sequence of hand-painted black musical notes, small and large eighth and sixteenth notes resembling trumpets, guitars, and trombones. Below, the stone steps looked secretly dark, dark enough to make Jack hesitate. Then again, where else could he go from here? The storm had made searching for Kate impossible. Until it passed, he was stranded, and so was she.

As he started down, the music washed over him, louder now, and he could make out applause for the saxophone solo, just ended, and a clear run of trumpet notes that might have been "Bye Bye Blackbird." Jack didn't know much jazz, but there were some songs, his father had said, that would last forever, no matter what else changed in the world.

It was the applause that made him most wary. How many graphically generated patrons would he find in the audience? Dared he believe anything he saw here after what happened at Paolo's? At the foot of the stairs was half a swing door, its twin broken and sagging by the hinges. Past that, he saw an illuminated bar, lit up with dark reds and muted golds that seemed to flicker through a wave of blue cigarette smoke, and a row of six or eight bar stools, all occupied by neopunks in studded leather, black suede, and long raincoats. None of them turned to stare as Jack strode in; their attention was fixed on the stage. As the trumpeter finished his short, sharp solo, the group lifted their hands to their chins, applauding.

Jack moved to the edge of the bar but stood slightly back from it, giving his eyes time to adjust to the light. A bartender saw him but didn't come over immediately. All around the room, the walls glowed with tiny, bright, electric candles, and something more—artwork of a kind Jack had never seen or imagined before. There were twenty or thirty abstract pictures in all, and each seemed alive, moving within its own frame. The colors of these fractals were stunning—golds, bottle-greens, and deep scarlets and blacks—and they shifted and redrew themselves constantly, in real time. Now and again, one or more of the fractals seemed painfully close to resembling something familiar; a face, a landscape, a sea urchin, a cloud formation; but then the similarity ended, the shapes reformed, the fractals became fractals again.

"What'll you have?" a voice called, jolting Jack out of his reverie. He'd been drifting miles away, transfixed by the artwork. The bartender faced him, his face as cold and vacant as the waitress in Paolo's. "What are you drinking, friend?"

"Just a Coke, thanks."

"Anything you say."

In three quick motions, the bartender wrenched a bottle from the cooler, uncapped it, and slid it across the bar in front of Jack.

"How much?" Jack asked. He was wondering about currency again, but the bartender shrugged and gestured across the room toward where another small group of neopunks huddled around a small table. "It's covered."

"By who?"

"Over there."

One of the group had stood up, and was waving Jack over. Jack had never seen the kid before in his life. Collecting the ice-cold bottle from the bar, he maneuvered his way around the barflies on stools, through patches of darkness, toward the table. As he reached the group, the kid who had summoned him—tall, goatee-bearded, dreadlocked, wearing wraparound shades—half grinned and said, "Human."

"How's that?"

"Sit down. I'll explain."

The others—a girl with thick, jet-black hair and a pale-painted face that gave her a ghostly, Gothic look, and two males, the first with a Mohawk and sharp, green eyes, the second dressed all in gray plastic and wearing tiny round shades—shuffled around the table to make way for Jack. He settled down just as the jazz band finished their number. The applause died, and a new song began, a quiet ballad led by the piano.

"Greg," the punk with the goatee said, extending his hand.

Jack shook it. "Greg Sharp? *The* Greg Sharp?"

"You're quick. The very same. My name must be legend already." He was grinning. "And this is Vern—" He waved a hand at the guy with the Mohawk. "And this here is Hal—" The punk in gray plastic never so much as glanced Jack's way. "And Janie."

"Jack North," Jack said, wetting his lips with the Coke. "You paid for this drink?"

"Not exactly. It's on our tab, but like everything else here the tab's just a kind of detail, there's no money involved, just the illusion of buying and selling, so we don't actually pay a cent," Greg said.

"Thanks anyway." Jack gazed, bewildered, around the table. Vern's piercing green eyes watched Jack intently; the girl, Janie, slurped noisily through a straw buried deep in a tumbler half filled with ice cubes and little else; the one called Hal stared straight ahead, unseeing, the flesh of his face in this light seeming as glossy and plastic as his clothes. "But what's happening here? You said something just then . . . you said *human*."

"*You're* human," Janie said. "That's what Greg meant. He can see them coming a mile away."

"You looked lost when you came in," Greg explained. "Took you a while to get your bearings. The . . . residents . . . never have that look. They *belong*."

"The residents?"

"That's right. Meaning everyone else."

"Like the girl in Paolo's?" Jack said.

"You've been there? Sure. Just like her. You don't have to look too hard to see what's phony and what's not in this place. Most of what you see around you is just decoration—the bartender, the drinkers at the bar, hell even the band." With a twist of the lips that might have been a grimace or a smile, he raised a glass to his lips. "I mean, Jack, this is my seventh *Scotch,* for Christ's sake. And believe me, it doesn't have any effect. I should know; I've tried hard enough."

124

"VR," Janie said, "still has a way to go."

"You're like me," Jack said on the edge of a sigh of relief. "You're all—"

"Human," the plastic-wrap punk said quickly before sealing his thin gray lips.

"Well, most of us are," Janie said. "One of us isn't. One of us sitting here is a man-machine, a resident here. Can you guess which?"

Jack looked across at the expressionless punk in plastic but said nothing. The others didn't seem to expect him to answer at once, so he took another sip from the Coke bottle. "You got trapped inside the game, too?" he asked.

"You betcha," Greg said. The wall lights diffracted in the lenses of his shades as he spoke. "Except, as you know, it's no game."

"I know what it isn't," Jack said. "It's what it *is* that's puzzling me."

"Well put," Vern said, slapping the table. He spoke loudly, eager to make himself heard above the music. "It's what programmers have been killing themselves for years to come up with. I read this article once called 'Into the Interface' or something like that, about the way operating systems were going . . . becoming more and more transparent, what with desktop VR and 3D video conferencing and so on, so that eventually what you'd end up with would be this guy sitting at some PC, interacting with others on the Net, or in his office or wherever, without so much as a thought as to how he was achieving all this. The computer has become more and more invisible, so invisible that now in your daily life it's hard to tell whether you're using one or not, whether you're tripping out through the screen or talking to people in the flesh."

"So which are we doing now?" Jack asked. "Are we really in Silicon Sphere, or sitting in front of our monitors?"

Greg Sharp said, "Caught in between, is my guess. The Sphere is trying to absorb us."

"Absorb us? How's that?"

"It's a gateway, not a game," Janie said. "The Sphere is kind of like Heaven with silicon chips and graphics accelerators. Or maybe Hell. Except we were *tricked* here. We were suckered inside, and we're not allowed back."

"But why?" Jack wanted to know. "What's the point of our being held prisoner?"

"Your guess is as good as mine," Greg said. "Someone has their reason. Some madman, probably. All *I* know is that I've been in and out of this place a dozen times over, back and forth, and each time it's been harder to get out than the last, and each time it seemed as if more and more traces of the Sphere escaped with me into the real world. As if I'd taken a part of this place home with me."

"A crack in reality," Vern said. "As the Sphere becomes more believable, the real world becomes less so. Even before I got stuck here, I'd been finding it harder and harder to tell the difference."

"But my family," Jack said, aghast. "My folks . . . all the

people I love are back there. What's going to happen to *them*?"

He badly wanted an answer to his question; a few reassuring words to dissolve the horror he was starting to feel. But when the others looked at each other, then quickly away, he knew that, deep down, their fears were exactly the same as his.

CHAPTER FOURTEEN

Later, while the storm cracked the black and red sky, the main street strobed through flickers of lightning. Dust clouds clung to the horizon; gusting wind bounced across the rooftops with a rhythm of fists. Huge yellow-gray balls of tumbleweed clogged the streets as Jack followed the four neopunks from the jazz bar back to Paolo's coffee shop, where the beta-version waitress, Natasha I.0B3, was still washing, drying, and stacking crockery. There were no other customers.

They took their places at a table near the door, and the waitress came over, bringing menus. While Jack um'd and ah'd over his order—he finally decided on coffee, and eggs Benedict—she regarded him blankly, as if seeing him for the very first time.

"She doesn't remember me," he said after she'd disappeared to the kitchen. "Are all the residents like her?"

Janie said, "You get the impression that they're basically brainless. I mean, very convincing as far as appearances go, but it's as if they're dead from the neck up. Like they're programmed to carry out a few simple tasks, but really can't think for themselves."

"When I was here before she seemed afraid of me, or of

128

something else. It came over her for only a second. And I thought—"

"You thought she was *almost* human," Vern said. "Well, every computer program has a personality; after all, humans *write* computer programs, and we leave a piece of ourselves inside everything we do, even every electronic thing. So in her case—" He paused until she'd placed their orders on the table and moved out of earshot again. "In her case, what you saw probably wasn't fear, but a quality someone had given her."

"Are you alone here, Jack?" Janie asked, spooning two, three sugars into her steaming black coffee. "Apart from us, I mean."

"I came with a friend. We came here together, but we were separated. There was a kind of a—"

"System freeze-up?" Greg said, second-guessing. "Tell me about it."

"At least that's how it seemed at the time. Her name was—is Kate Kreuger. I lost her at the hotel."

"We were there, too," Janie said. "That's how Greg and I got parted, but we found each other at Alphazone. So there's hope for you yet."

Alphazone, Jack remembered, was one of the names mentioned in the scribbled notes he and Kate had found. "What happened?"

"We were up on the hotel's second floor," Greg said, tugging on his goatee. "Can't remember which of the rooms we were in, but things were pretty damn strange in there, even before I lost Janie. I'd been using a touchpad to control our movements, forward and back and so on, and suddenly I found I didn't need it at all; I looked down and realized I wasn't even touching it, and we were able to move and pick up objects with our bare hands. Just like now." He lifted his coffee cup from the table, set it down with a thump. "See how we've started to take stuff like this for granted so soon? It's a goddamn miracle, in my humble opinion. Anyway, in the room we were in, we'd tuned into a TV station where some kid began talking to us through interference. It was as if someone had pulled the plug but the picture was still coming through, and this kid—"

"He looked a little like Greg," Janie said. "We couldn't see his eyes. He was bald. He wore shades. He sounded scared as hell."

"I saw him, too," Jack said. "Same thing."

"He kept talking about Alphazone," Greg said. "He sounded frantic. He'd been going for two or three minutes—couldn't hear half of what he said because of the TV noise—and then suddenly, it was like—"

"Like an earthquake," Janie said. "It felt like something rocking the room."

"Truth is, I thought we'd been struck by lightning," Greg said. "But when lightning takes out your transmission you'd expect the TV to blank out." He took a quick sip of his coffee. "It didn't happen like that. What happened was, the TV picture, the *image*, exploded into the room. The noise, the snow, everything except the dude we'd been listening to."

130

"The TV snow was everywhere," Janie said. "It filled the room, bouncing off walls, millions of multicolored, tiny specks of blue and green and red lights. I felt it prickling my face and hands. I cried out. I don't remember what happened after that. The next thing I knew—"

"I saw it all," Greg said before she could finish. "I saw Janie covered from head to foot in electrons, staggering about, thrashing her arms, leaving streaks of light behind her as she moved, and for a second it looked as if she was made out of these dots, *composed* of them, you know, no more substantial than a TV picture herself. I tried to grab hold of her but my hand passed right through where her arm should have been. It was just empty space. I heard her scream, but her voice seemed to come from far away. There was a surge of electricity that knocked me to the floor, took my breath away. By the time I looked up the snow had sucked itself back inside the TV, and Janie was gone.

"For a while I kept flicking channels on TV, half expecting her to show up there. I was starting to panic; I guess this was the point I stopped thinking of Silicon Sphere as a game. Then I thought, wherever that kid is, that's where Janie is, too. Alphazone. It was marked on a circuitboard map on the wall. That was when I ran out of the hotel."

"I think I heard you," Jack said, remembering a figure darting breathlessly past the room he had entered during his first journey to the Sphere. To Janie he said, "What happened to you?"

"I woke up in what I guessed was a cell, because the windows were locked, but not barred, and the glass looked about two inches thick. Down below I could see what looked like a big industrial complex—low, flat, rectangular blocks with mirror windows, and guys in white uniforms standing guard. I couldn't tell whether they had weapons or not. At the far side of the complex there was a building with a dome; a huge, gorgeous dome that looked like it was made out of crystal . . ."

"Hell, from the road it looked like much more than that," Greg said. "I was driving up there in a Chevy I'd found parked in a side street near Pablo One. The route to Alphazone takes you way into the desert, miles from anywhere. From a mile or so away, I could see the sun glinting off the dome. Nearer, I didn't know *what* to make of it. The building was textured, covered in relief patterns, all highs and lows and shadowy contours: *This is way cool,* I remember thinking. It looked like . . . like a *brain* made of crystal. I swear."

There was a lull while Greg contemplated what he had seen and Jack tried to picture it for himself. "The other buildings," Jack said, turning it Janie. "Have you any idea what they were?"

Janie shrugged. The muscles of her face had tightened. "I could only guess at the time. The whole place had an antiseptic feel, like a science lab. I got the impression I'd been taken there for a reason; if Greg hadn't shown up when he did I'm sure I would've found out what the hard way."

"The compound was fenced off at the perimeter," Greg

132

said. "I stopped the car and got out to take a closer look. I could see the guards, but they didn't seem to see me; my feeling was they'd been posted there for show, to deter snoopers like me, but I couldn't be sure they weren't dangerous. A hundred or so yards from the car I found a gap in the fence where the wire had been cut. I dodged through—there were no guards in that part of the complex—and headed to the nearest block for cover, keeping close to the walls. The blocks were so close together, I could dodge between them easily without being seen. The glass was tinted dark, so I couldn't see inside, but I still had the feeling of being watched; as if whoever was in charge there had allowed me to walk right in . . ."

"It must have been pure chance," Janie said, "but I was looking out from the cell just as Greg cut between two of the blocks. I wanted to shout—hell, I wanted to scream at the top of my voice—but I felt sure I'd be playing into their hands if I did. Instead, I could only hope he'd look up. Even then, I had serious doubts about what would happen if he *did* see me—there was no way of knowing whether my building was crawling with guards." Janie drew a deep breath, clutching briefly at Greg's hand. "Then I thought, but hey, suppose this really is some kind of game . . . just think of all the Dungeons and Dragons scenarios we've played down the years, rescuing the fair maiden from the tower, overcoming the gremlins and evil sorcerers. Maybe this is nothing more than Dungeons and Dragons with a super-real modern twist. And so when Greg came into view again, I started yelling and hammering the glass with both fists."

"I heard her but I didn't see her at first," Greg said. "I could pick out the thump-thump-thump on the window, and I could tell it was coming from somewhere high up. Even when I looked up, all I could see was floor upon floor of darkened windows and, way above me, a sort of pale shape standing in one of them; it could've been anything, but I wanted to believe it was her.

"There was a large courtyard and almost no cover between where I was standing and the main building, so I didn't expect to get there unseen. I started toward it, and almost immediately I heard a siren."

"That was when I became really afraid," Janie said. "The trap had been set, I'd drawn Greg neatly into it, and—"

"Before I knew what hit me," Greg said, "there were three or four guards on my case. They came out of nowhere, seizing my arms, jabbing rifles into my ribs, frogmarching me into the building. Inside were more guards, all dressed in gray, all of them armed, their faces completely blank. They were standing in a foyer that looked like it was made of stainless steel, the floors and ceiling, everything. There were hundreds of spotlights in the ceiling shining straight down, but the overall impression I got was of darkness. Across the way I saw a bank of elevators, and even before they marched me toward them I knew that's where I was going. The guards who'd caught me outside left me with the others and headed, I guessed, back to their posts.

The rest—four of them—bundled me into one of the elevators." Greg broke off for a moment, idly scratching his brow, frowning. Outside, the wind rose and fell, whispering. "No one spoke. I guess even if they had, I wouldn't have been less intimidated, but there wasn't a flicker of communication between them, and still they all seemed to know what to do automatically.

"When we reached the floor—I don't remember which one—the elevator stopped and the doors opened and ahead of us I saw a long corridor with rows of steel doors. From somewhere along there I could hear muffled noises, someone bashing the window and crying; I knew it had to be Janie. I said something then . . . I can't remember exactly . . . 'Stop this now, will you? Will you please stop this now?' The panic was setting in. There was no way back once they'd locked me in one of those rooms; I was certain. This wasn't a game and it hadn't been since the beginning. Silicon Sphere was the bait to lure us into this hell, and I didn't want to know what happened here; I really wasn't curious anymore."

For a moment Greg looked distraught, still reliving the moment. Then he said, "I can't say what went through my mind at that point, but the next thing I knew I'd launched myself at one of the guards, knocking him off balance, trying to wrestle the rifle from him. It was a crazy thing to do, I know, totally crazy, but I'd almost stopped caring. Everything happened real fast after that.

"First, I felt a rifle butt catch me somewhere about here."

135

Greg's fingertips brushed his right shoulder. "In fact it hit me like a ton of goddamn bricks and I felt the dizziness wash right over me. Then I was being dragged away from him, backward, out of the elevator, by one of the other guards. The three who were still inside were raising their weapons toward me, and I thought, *Okay, that was dumb, really dumb, what you just did; and see how far it's gotten you now?* I think I probably closed my eyes, waiting for the bullets to fly, or maybe I didn't even get *that* far, because that was when Hal pushed me aside and fired three or four quick shots into the elevator."

"Hal?" Jack North's attention drifted from Greg to the punk sitting next to him. "Are you talking about *this* Hal?"

"The very same." Greg smiled and visibly relaxed. "That was the moment me and Hal met. Hal was my savior; the fourth armed guard."

Hal continued to gaze into space, his face unreadable, eyes hidden behind shades. After a moment he turned slightly toward Jack. "I was like you once," he said flatly. "Part of me still is. A very small part."

"Meaning what?" Jack said.

"I'll explain." At first Greg came forward slowly, drawing his chair to the table with a screech. Then, in one swift movement, he brought up his right hand, taking Hal firmly by the collar, forcing him face downward until his face brushed the table's surface. Before Jack could react, Greg had seized what looked a flap of loose skin at the nape of Hal's head for all to see.

136

Jack watched in awe; he was staring, he thought, at a minute engine, all ribbons and cables and blinking neon lights. It reminded him of a miniature city, a version of the circuit board map on the hotel room wall. Reaching inside, Greg touched a small metal jumper and Hal shivered and lay still, a faint regular bleep rising from the back of his skull like a pulse.

"See here?" Greg said. "I'm no expert—I mean I couldn't *build* one of these things—but there are several loose connections. It's my guess that Hal blew a fuse, literally. He'd been programmed to do a job for *them,* whoever they are, but malfunctioned and turned against them."

"What is he?" Jack said. "Man or machine?" He cast a wary glance toward Natasha I.0B3, who was watching from the counter, expressionless. "Is he like her?"

"Hard to say without opening her up as well," Vern said. "What we can be sure of is that there's human tissue in here. See this? And this? But whichever Hal was to begin with, right now he's both man *and* machine."

Jack sat in bemused silence, his heart racing. Outside, a peal of thunder sounded sampled, an electronic imitation of the real thing. Beads of rain patted the door at the entrance. "We still don't know why Hal turned," Greg said. "It could've been something as simple as a failed interrupt request, an overheating chip in the CPU—"

"Or maybe just a good old-fashioned nervous breakdown," Janie said. "Either way, the answer is probably buried in here somewhere, in the on-board memory. We'd probably learn a lot about Hal, and this place, if we could find a way to tap into this circuitry."

Greg clicked the jumper inside Hal's head and Hal flickered to life again.

"Hal?" Janie said.

Hal remained face down on the table with Greg's prying fingers still touching his circuitry.

"Hal," he said, as if remembering his name. "Final release one-oh-vee-one. Checking memory: thirty-six gigabytes in use, thirty-two terabytes free. Memory test successful. Welcome. Welcome."

"He's booting up just like a goddam PC," Vern whispered.

"Do you hear me, Hal?" Janie said.

"I hear you."

"Do you know who we are?"

"You're like me. You're human. That is Janie speaking; voice pattern logged."

"Showing your true colors now," Greg said. "Hal, you say that you're human. But *are* you human? I mean, are you really like us?"

There was a long wait during which Jack began to think Hal had stopped functioning. Then Hal said, "Auto-check commencing. Scanning . . . Scanning . . . Testing for overwritten data. Testing encrypted data. Check complete: for full details, see report."

"Read the report, Hal," Vern said quickly.

Again, the electronic pulse kept them waiting. "Analyzing report," Hal said. "Signs of human life found prior to re-format. Report ends."

"Jesus." Jack was leaning forward across the table, his whole body tense as a tourniquet. "Did he just say *reformat? Does* that mean what I think it does?"

He hoped it didn't; he would have given anything to believe otherwise. While Greg rezipped Hal's skull, Natasha I.0B3 continued about her business, clearing and clattering cups and saucers, oblivious.

"You can bet that it does," Janie said at long last. "He was human once, and so was she. And then someone—something, maybe—decided to rebuild them, wipe out all the old data, throw out the old technology, build in the new." The muscles of her face looked drawn and tight as she added, "And that's what would've become of us if we'd stayed any longer. If Hal hadn't turned, we would've been company for him."

"And Kate . . ." Jack felt and sounded close to hysteria. His voice wavered, hoarse and wafer thin, close to a shriek. "What about Kate?"

The others heard him but at first didn't look at him. Perhaps they couldn't; they had already seen what he could only imagine.

"Would you go there again?" Jack asked. "Would you at least show me the way to Alphazone?"

Janie tried to force a smile, hoping to reassure him, but it faded quickly, and an uncomfortable silence spun out.

CHAPTER FIFTEEN

The storm was rising beautifully to its peak, and now, to top it all, *they* were coming: his children were nearly home.

While a few short miles away, Jack North and four neo-punks were piling into the old green Chevy, Eddie Matrix looked out across Silicon Sphere from the warmth of his den, marveling at how things would be when the crack in the world opened wide.

It was only a matter of time. Already the world was transforming, so slowly it would take a trained eye to see the change. Already there were outlets here and there in reality, holes through which Eddie's dream was slowly escaping; but as yet these were small rivulets rather than great gaping rivers—games and TV shows and VR headsets—that would seem very slight when the flood began. These smart, turned-on, tuned-in kids would become his messengers, spreading the virtual word. It would be their mission to change the world. And they would change their world gladly, once they'd seen the light.

The storm was just the way he'd hoped it would be. Great red clouds swarmed across the horizon like ghosts, blotting out a purple neon moon; forks of lightning danced nervously, bleaching the Alphazone courtyard white. It felt good, he thought, to command such raw power, to have learned so soon how to apply it.

He sat at a large maple desk, a Matrix Mark II laptop nestling at his hands, watching the storm's rise and fall on his screen. In the bottom left corner of the screen was a 3D rendered image of a face he knew only too well: Leon Speakes. It was a face he had pinned, once or twice, to a virtual dartboard; but darts made of pixels were harmless, and therefore no fun. He wanted to see Speakes cringe and plead in the flesh. The thief's day was over, and Speakes would be well advised to make the most of the time he had left while he could. Whenever he looked at Speakes's face, thunder clapped.

Speakes was still out there, of course, raking in big bucks for Vanguard Systems, his personal fortune standing somewhere between six and eight billion dollars. *Soon,* Matrix thought, *that fortune will be dust, gone with the storm, and then we'll see who's king and who's pawn in this game . . .*

It was at a desk very much like this that he'd first sat face to face with Leon Speakes. By then, Matrix had already been in Cupertino three weeks, where he'd joined the Vanguard 2 development unit. It felt like an insult: here he was, working on somebody else's behalf to "improve" what he'd already perfected the first time around, and—worse—being asked to change and even throw out great chunks of code that he'd written himself. Leon Speakes might have been a hotshot in business, but at the creative level, he was basically clueless. Having stolen the prize, the thief had proceeded to ruin it.

Then again, Eddie Matrix had not joined Vanguard to help out; he'd gone there to bring down the empire, to destroy it forever. In the end, of course, it hadn't turned out that way; nothing ever worked out the way you intended. Maybe Speakes had known all along who he was really employing—after all, he and Eddie had video-conferenced for long enough on the Internet; Speakes had seen Eddie's face, even though Eddie had seen only Natasha's.

Speakes must've suspected *something*.

During those first weeks on the Vanguard 2 project, Eddie felt sure he was being watched. Sometimes his e-mail arrived too late, hours—rather than seconds—after being posted. Once, he thought he heard a double click on the line as he spoke on the phone to his folks back home.

Maybe it was just paranoia: after all, there he was, working late, hammering out code alone long after the rest of the team had signed out and gone home. He spent several evenings building a complex series of system subroutines into the software; a bug here, a Trojan Horse there. Certain combinations of these, he knew, had the potential to trash any computer that ran the software. All were configured to trigger weeks from now, after the launch of Vanguard 2, so no one would ever suspect him; it was like making a time bomb.

If only a handful of lethal bugs made it through the final

release, it wouldn't be long before complaints started flooding the company's help lines. There would be hardware damage and data loss on a scale never known or seen before. Entire information databases worldwide would be wiped out. Whole corporations would come crashing down. Banks would lose billions of dollars. The lawsuits would follow, and with Leon Speakes' reputation in tatters, the company in ruins, Eddie would add insult to injury, making the theft of Matrix OS public knowledge.

No wonder he felt watched; no wonder he was living in fear. If Speakes ever got wind of what he was up to . . .

Which was why his mouth ran dry the morning the e-mail pinged in his in box; it was an invitation to lunch with Speakes himself. "Lucky you," marveled Lauren, a secretary, sneaking a glance at Eddie's screen as she dumped the morning snail mail on his desk. "I've been here six months and I haven't had so much as a 'come take a memo.' Hell, you can't be much more than seventeen. I'll bet you only just started shaving. What've you got that I haven't?"

Eddie shrugged, as though he really didn't have the slightest idea, but in truth he was worried. He had an insider's knowledge; a knowledge that could prove dangerous to Speakes. He'd realized only too well, the day he stepped on the Greyhound bus to Cupertino, that he was gambling everything for a chance to get even. It was worth the gamble, but Speakes was smart; you had to get up pretty early in the morning to catch this particular worm.

Maybe, Eddie thought at the time, closing the in box and returning to work, *maybe this really is the end of the line.*

Now, in his office in Silicon Sphere, his clawed hands tensed at the edge of his desk as he remembered the meeting again. In one way, yes, that lunchtime showdown *had* been the end of the line; but in another way, it had signaled a new beginning. If not for Speakes, he wouldn't be here now, in the virtual world. He wouldn't have *made* this world.

He remembered Speakes sitting with his back to the window, beyond which the hazy Californian sky met the green swathe of parkland, all fountains and tall bronze sculptures imported from England. The light was low, hard, and dull and shone straight into Eddie Matrix's eyes, making him squint. He guessed Speakes had it planned that way, to make him feel like a suspect trapped in a police interrogation.

But Speakes' voice—he could barely see his face, for the backlighting had turned Speakes into a silhouette—was patient and calm. And very young, Eddie thought. Speakes couldn't be much older than himself.

"I guess you know why I asked to see you, Eddie," he began. "And I can guess why you applied to work here at Vanguard. Which, in a way, makes us even."

"Not exactly," Eddie said. "You own the company. I just work for it."

Speakes made a dry rasping sound; maybe a laugh. "Very

good, but what I mean is, we both know a little more about each other than we're pretending, don't we?"

"How so?"

"Please, Eddie, don't play games with me. I know who you are, because no one gets to work here *without* me knowing who they are. Besides which, I know about your visit to San Francisco. You came by to see if Natasha was home. And of course you found out that she wasn't."

Speakes sat perfectly still, waiting, the fingers of his right hand brushing imaginary specks from his desk.

Eddie knew there was no point in keeping up the pretense. It had always been in the cards that Speakes would find him out; he'd just hoped it would take slightly longer than this. His best bet now would be to admit his plans—admit that he'd come to Cupertino for revenge—and hope the bugs he'd already coded into the project would go undetected. "Natasha was a wonderful creation," he said finally. "It took me a while to get over her."

"I could tell you took her seriously. I'm sorry, for your sake, she wasn't real." At least Speakes sounded fairly sincere. "I didn't mean to hurt your feelings; I'd created her and I wanted to get some feedback, to see how people out there reacted to her. I never expected to hook someone like you."

"Like me?"

"Someone with your genius. Built-in, natural-born, knock-em-dead genius. I'm being perfectly honest with you,

Eddie. I never saw anyone who could program like you. I never could have done what you've done. That's why when you uploaded your software to my desktop, I couldn't resist—"

Now we're getting somewhere, Eddie thought.

"I couldn't resist helping myself," Speakes went on. "I was taking an opportunity, the kind of opportunity we're lucky to see once in a lifetime, and it turned out to be my passport."

"Well, it left *me* in the dust," Eddie said testily.

Speakes was nodding in full agreement. "I know how it seems. It looks like theft—on paper I suppose it is just that—but where were you really going, Eddie? I mean, you were so naïve, you uploaded your work to a complete stranger."

"I didn't believe Natasha was a complete stranger. She seemed real enough at the time."

"That's not the point I'm making. What I'm saying is, you don't have a head for business. I do. You're a brilliant programmer—I've never seen anyone like you before—but you'd never have seen your operating system in the real world without me."

"Okay, so now I see it. And it has your name on it."

"Only because I'm running the show now. Cool down for a minute, Eddie, and think. Use your head. Do you honestly believe I'd let someone with your gift hack out a living as you are right now and take no credit for what you've done? I've got plans for you; that's why you're up here talking to me now. No one comes through that door unless I want them to. No, this isn't to clear the air, although I hope we can manage that too. Bottom line is, I want you to join me."

Eddie watched the still, dark silhouette across the desk with an air of bemusement. "Join you? Join you in what?"

"Get up, go out the door, and take a look in the office next door. Then tell me what you think."

"Is this some kind of game?"

"No. Just do it." Speakes motioned him away. "Go ahead. Don't be shy."

Okay, Eddie thought. *Something's brewing here. Just do what he says. At least don't step out of line until you know what the rules are.*

He got up, crossed the thickly carpeted floor, stepped out of the office and turned to his immediate right. The next door along was just another clone office door: he hesitated outside it, wondering whether—just maybe—a crack team of hitmen would take him out the minute he stepped inside. But that was a crazy notion: someone as powerful as Speakes could do what he liked to anyone, whenever he wanted, and far more discreetly than that.

The office next door was empty. It was almost a duplicate of the office he'd just left—plush, with large abstract prints on the walls, a huge maple desk, a view of the parkland, the works.

"So do you like it?" Speakes asked, suddenly behind him.

"Sure, but I don't see —"

"It's yours."

Eddie looked at him, aghast. Then he looked at the room; then at Speakes. "All right. Dream's over. Just pinch me and I'll wake up."

"No dream, no joke. I'm offering you something you probably *couldn't* have dreamed," Speakes said calmly. "We're moving Vanguard forward in a big way. There's something new on the agenda, something that really *will* change the world, and I want you on board. In fact I'd like you to head up the project. Just imagine, if we pool our resources, where we'll be in a year from now."

Well, now we know, Eddie thought now, watching the courtyard at Alphazone. *No, it wasn't a dream, but even if it began as one, over time it became a nightmare.*

I'll tell you where we're going," Speakes told him over lunch, the day after that first meeting. "With Matrix OS, the first Vanguard operating system, and now with Vanguard 2, we have an interface that actually means something to ordinary people who use the personal computer. Everything behaves the way we expect it to; it learns from us, and we learn from it. . . . Except we don't have to learn about what lies underneath. We don't need to know the technology. We can speak with it, tell it what to do, ask it how we do such and such—it's an almost human response, okay?"

"Well, that was what I always liked about it," Eddie said. "I mean, I stole from the best, and came up with something new."

"That's how we progress. But the problem with this way of working," Speakes went on, "is that it's all external. It only uses *some* of our senses. That's what I want to over-come with the new project."

Eddie took a sip of ice water and aligned his knife and fork on the plate. The smoked salmon salad had been ex-quisite; the restaurant, with its tall, indoor palm trees and silvery fountains, was unlike any he'd been in before.

"Could you explain?" he wondered. "How far do you want to go? What do you want exactly?"

Speakes bunched nearer across the table, excited. "How about immortality, for starters? A place in history? This isn't just about big bucks, Ed, though it is about that, too. I want to see total immersion. Up until now what we've had is us and them, us and computers, us and machines, whatever. We've been growing closer together for decades now, and ever since the first VR headset I saw at some Expo years ago, I've been a believer. What we want, what *I* want, and I'm damn sure what everyone else wants, too, is one more big step in the same direction. In other words, a fusion."

"A fusion?"

"A coming together of us and them. Why else would we want VR or nanotechnology or bionics? It's where we've been heading all along, ever since the Industrial Revolution got rolling. Just think of the changes you've seen in *your* lifetime—and I'll bet the day you were born there were al-ready talking car alarms on the streets."

"Yes, there were, I think."

"So now we have in-car security mechanisms that will accept your voice print and password. If you don't know the password, you can't steal the sucker. We have VCRs that you can *tell* what to record and when. That's kids' stuff. And we have interactive this and interactive that, and electronic hearts and kidneys that you can get, if you can afford them and you want to keep living a few more years. Nowadays, even our bodily parts are just items you can pick from a shelf. Nose jobs and boob jobs and lipo and facelifts were old hat even decades ago. Hell, I could write you a list, but it'd take forever, and I'm already late for a meeting. Fact is, ten years from now it won't be the way it is today: there'll be no more computers, and no more *us*. We're going to combine ourselves, we're going to become one, and you, Eddie Matrix, from Noplace, Nevada, are going to make sure that we do it right."

He spoke like a man possessed, Eddie thought. Later, he remembered the look in Speakes' eyes as he preached the New Thing. Maybe Jehovah's Witnesses wore the same look in the days they came buzzing your door before they started evangelizing via the Net. In any case, there was something about Speakes' vision that he couldn't resist. Maybe it was a cold view of the future, or maybe it was just that the future was destined to *be* cold, and Speakes was just facing facts, but it sounded about right, and it felt right to Eddie. He thought it over for a couple of weeks, then decided.

He was up for it.

■　■　■

The surgery lasted less than an hour, they told him. At first, he hadn't known there would be such a thing as surgery, but there was no discomfort involved, even though Speakes had joked earlier that there was "never any progress without pain." The surgeon called the operation a refit.

"From the outside, you look just like you did before," he said. Then he gave Eddie Matrix a wink.

They gave him forty-eight hours to let the anesthetic wear off, and then Speakes phoned him at home. He sounded jubilant, younger than ever, his voice cracking as if it was set to break.

"They say it went like a dream, Ed. Do you feel any different? How are your thoughts?"

"About the same just now. Except—"

"Yes? Yes?"

"It must be the drugs they gave me. I feel like I know things that I really shouldn't know—y'know, phone numbers, grocery prices. I haven't quite focused on anything else yet."

"Those figures are supposed to be there," Speakes said. "The nanochip they implanted contains a few sample databases—phone books and such. Can you give me my Uncle Walt's address in Wisconsin? His name is Fry; Walter Julius Fry."

"Sure, that's 220 Vale Street. You want the zip too?" Eddie said this without thinking; the information came automatically. Then it hit him. "What *is* that? How could I know that?"

"Just to give you a taste of what's in store," Speakes said. "Okay, that's a pretty lame example—you *are* carrying several gigabytes worth of directories around in your head—but it's only the tip of the iceberg. The chip is upgradeable, for one thing. We can feed new information into it or replace it with a newer model, when one comes along. But right now, believe me, you are like no other man. You're the first in line, Ed, the first of the New Vanguard. Just think of that, and sleep on it. Then come see me in my office in the morning."

It took Eddie a while to be comfortable about the implant. Previously, he had needed a high-powered PC with a math coprocessor to work out the complex calculations he could now do instantly in his head. He knew every name and number in a dozen phone books without thinking about it; every definition in the complete Oxford English Dictionary.

During the first month following the operation, he sat in on board meetings, gave lectures at computer shows, provided *Time* magazine with an interview that made the front page. This time it was his face, not Speakes', that made the cover. He was moving up.

A small but significant metal jack socket had been implanted at the back of his neck. This bothered him at first, until Speakes explained what it was for. "That's how we keep you up to date. Instead of performing surgery each time the chip is upgraded, we just plug you in and zap you with a flash ROM update. You like that? Okay, so each time we develop new technologies or improve old ones, or each time the stock market fluctuates, that's how we feed the information to you. You can jack yourself into the Internet, say two or three times a day, and download the latest information from there. Then the next stop is to get you programming using this link. We want you and the machine to become one. That's the way forward. What do you think?"

Eddie knew, deep down, this was what he'd been searching for. Long ago, in his father's den, he'd found himself by escaping the world. He'd sold his soul to techno. Now the escape was complete.

"It's like Adam and Eve," he said. "Just me and the computer, and whatever comes next."

And Leon Speakes smiled.

But the headaches began once he really got working. Each day, following eight hours wired up to the latest, hottest computer hardware, he retired to bed with red and yellow-purple flashes behind his eyes. When he put on the night-light and opened his eyes, the flashes were still there in his room. For a while, at first, his nights were restless; but when he did sleep, he dreamed weird, silent, multicolored dreams in which he traveled across skies made of shimmering, molten chrome, walked desolate streets lined with dust-blown villas. Awake, wherever he went, he saw neon in everything.

It went on like this for a time, but he kept his worries to himself. Perhaps it was just a case of getting used to it, coming to terms with what he'd become. Besides, the project was too important to compromise for the sake of a few small migraines. He didn't want Leon to postpone or cancel. So in a daze he worked, dreamed, and slept, and dreamed, slept and worked until it became harder and harder to distinguish which was which at any one time. When the headaches surged at him, he resisted, telling himself, *You're the first, remember, the first in line. The first of the New. You were born for this.*

So don't blow it.

The day he really got scared, the day the sky came crashing down, was the day every member of a board meeting he was attending turned into molten metal. By then it was far too late to go back.

He was sitting opposite Speakes at the meeting and between two representatives from the sales division. There was a lot of discussion about productivity and quarterly losses and gains that he didn't take any interest in—which was why his attention drifted. While the sales reps talked he began watching Speakes' personal secretary, who was frantically taking minutes for the meeting on a yellow legal pad in shorthand. *Install the chip, a microphone and software,* he thought, *and shorthand will be obsolete too. She'll just know everything that was said here.*

He noticed she was writing with a slim chrome-plated pen. It fit her hand snugly. She had small, delicate hands. Her nails were polished in a sparkling gray that matched the pen.

He looked again, and felt another of the multicolored migraines looming.

It wasn't only her nail polish that matched, but her hand as well; her whole hand, and the arm it belonged to. In fact, for the first time, he saw her for what she really was: a secretary made out of metal. But that was nothing; that was only a brief impression. The fact of the matter was, she was melting. She was sitting there, taking minutes, melting into a pool of hot chrome on the table. Should he scream for help?

In panic, Eddie Matrix scanned the table.

The only reason no one else there had noticed or commented was that the board members—every last one of them—had begun to melt, too.

He woke up in a chair in his office. He had no idea how much later, or how he'd found his way there. When his vision cleared he saw Speakes, who was perched on the edge of the desk, not melting, just smiling, as usual. Then again this wasn't his usual smile, the smile of a born-again technofiend. This smile was a smug, victorious tilt of the lips that for no reason he could think of made Eddie's blood run cold.

"It's beginning, isn't it?" Speakes said after a time. He was surrounded by a weird amber glow.

"I . . . nnhh . . . Didn't you . . . Didn't you see what happened back there?"

"I saw the spectacle you made of yourself. We all did."

"You didn't see?"

"We saw you freaking out like some drug-warped hippie. Eddie, you have no *idea* . . . I mean, I just wish I'd video-taped the meeting. You were really quite something."

"I don't . . . don't understand . . . what's happening to me . . ."

Eddie stood, or at least tried to stand, and as he did the floor flashed up toward him. Somehow, in a mass of tangled limbs, he found himself at Speakes' feet, down on all fours, the room strobing at the edges of his vision with quick bright static flashes.

"You don't know?" Speakes said. "But then how could you? You've never been this far before. All right, Ed, I'll tell you. I'll tell you what's happening. But please don't ask if there's anything I can do to help."

"It's the implant," Eddie said. To his ears, his own voice sounded farther away than Speakes', even though that was an echo. "It has something to do with this thing in my head."

"Correct."

"Is it defective? Am I dying?"

"No you're not. Not exactly. But I suppose you could say that you're blowing out."

Eddie peered, half blind, at the figure perched on the desk above him. He could only see stars, splitting and mutating like fractals. "How . . . how exactly do you mean?"

"We know what you're here for," Speakes said. "We know why you came in the first place. Please don't think that you're so far ahead of the rest of us that we're unable to see what you're trying to do to our project. I know your only real motive is to wreck Vanguard 2, and I know about every virus and Trojan Horse you built into it. I know, for Chrissakes, that you came here to ruin me. Did you expect me to sit here and take it?"

"But that . . . was then. I thought we'd cleared the air. What about . . . what about the new project?"

"Do you really believe I'd waste something as big as this on you? You were always such a child, Eddie. I mean, giving away the Matrix OS like that to a girl in cyberspace—that's the mark of a complete novice. You still have a hell of a lot to learn."

"So why?"

"Because I wanted to settle our account. It's paid in full, and the balance is inside your head, my friend. Is it giving you headaches? I thought so. Bad dreams? That's nothing to what they'll become."

Eddie was staring up at Speakes in sheer horror. His senses were clearing, but only enough to deepen his panic. "What have you done? What have you done? What *is* this thing?"

"It's exactly as I described it. It's a very advanced nano-chip, less than half the size of your thumbnail, and you can use it in every way I explained. Thing is, Ed, it carries more than the data I told you about. We plugged a few of your Trojan Horses in there for good measure."

That was the moment the world fell out from beneath Eddie Matrix's feet. He had known terror before, in small doses—terror of bullies at school, of street gangs, of being found out in Cupertino—but never, before or since, anything like that. It was the very worst case scenario. The viruses in his head were designed to destroy entire information systems, to bring corporations the size of Vanguard to their knees. In his wisdom, he hadn't seen fit to write an antidote. It was the moment he knew he was finished.

He left Cupertino on a Greyhound bus just the way he'd arrived, but he didn't head back to his parents in Nowhereville. There would be no way to explain how he had changed, or how—God help him—he would continue to change. The knowledge would kill them. It was one thing to have merged with the machine; quite another to have merged with a machine that was crippled by binary plagues.

He had money, enough to get by with, and a length of jack cable to fit the socket at the back of his neck. He decided that, for now, that was all he would need. He headed out to the desert, took a room at some remote motel outside of Las Vegas, drew the blinds, and plugged himself into the modem. There, remote from the world but still connected, he began to dream.

CHAPTER SIXTEEN

Roy McKee finally caught up with Alison Dougan in the staff parking lot right after school. She had the driver's door of her Fiesta wedged open and was slinging a black briefcase onto the back seat. Above the school's gray, cell-like blocks, the sky was darkening to a deep violet-red hue. The clouds which had been massing all afternoon glowed like neon. Across the far side of the parking lot, watched by a throng of excitable fifth graders, two BBC newsmen were taping an interview with the school principal.

"Alison?" Roy said.

At first she seemed unable to place him. A tired, glazed cast slowly cleared from her eyes.

"Roy, I'm sorry. I was miles away."

"That's okay. I'm getting used to it."

"How's that?"

"I don't mean from you, I mean generally. Everyone seems so distracted these days."

"I know what you mean. If they aren't distracted, they're just plain absent. Where is everyone, Roy? What's happening here?"

"That's what I wanted to talk to you about."

"You know where they are?—Kyle and Kate and Jack?"

"I have an idea. I think it has some connection with Silicon Sphere."

"Oh." She seemed to know what he meant at once. "Look, I'm just leaving. Can I drop you off somewhere? We'll talk along the way."

"Anywhere near town would be fine. Thanks."

He waited while she unlocked the passenger door, then climbed inside. The floor mat felt gritty under his shoes, and on the dash there were grains of something that looked like wet sand. "You've been to the beach?" he asked.

"No, not for a long time. This sand, whatever it is, seems to be everywhere lately. At first I thought it was in the air, but now I'm beginning to wonder . . ."

"Wonder what?"

"An oddball notion, that's all. You were saying about your friends . . . You do know the police have been here today, don't you?"

"Yeah, and the press. I didn't speak to *them,* but the cops dragged me out of an English class and asked about Jack and Kate and Kyle, but there was nothing I could tell them—nothing that would've made much sense, anyway."

Alison edged the Fiesta into gear. The engine was cold, and they shuddered to the junction in nervous steps. "You make that sound as though you might have told them something but chose not to."

"I would've, if I thought it would help."

"I see. So what *didn't* you tell the police?"

160

"What do you know about Silicon Sphere?" he asked.

"What can I tell you? It's what you'd call way cool, I suppose. Oddly enough, Jack asked me exactly the same question before he and Kyle started missing classes and then disappeared, period. All I can say is I've played it. I've been there."

"We've all been there," Roy said. "Thing is, I'm not sure all of us came back."

Alison shot him a narrow-eyed look while she waited for the traffic to clear. "Are you saying what I think you're saying?"

"Let me try to explain."

"I think you'd better."

He told her about it while she drove—the whole story up to and including last night, when instead of heading home from school he'd continued on the bus straight to Jack's. He hadn't been sure that was a good idea, but he felt compelled: perhaps he'd be able to spot something the police had missed.

He'd expected to find Jack's family in shock, but at least they weren't frantic. If anything, they seemed oddly subdued, as if someone had been feeding them tranquilizers. Through most of his stay, Jack's mother and father sat in the living room gazing at the TV. They spoke to Roy in fragile, faraway voices, like mourners. Oddly, he thought, they never switched off the TV; maybe they were watching for news reports.

Jack's sister, Sandy, had answered the door looking tight-lipped and pale. She'd lost the glow Roy had seen on her the last time they'd met. Her boyfriend was with her, a guy called Dan Morrisey. A tall, dark-haired business type in his early or mid-twenties, he wore a suit that looked like money and shook Roy's hand firmly, though his face remained troubled and set.

"He works for DataLite, as a programmer," Sandy said proudly. It was the only time her eyes seemed to light up. "He's been great about all of this. I don't know what I would've done without him."

"Could I see Jack's room?" Roy said to Sandy. "I thought perhaps it might tell me something."

"Like what? That he isn't there?" Quickly she reached out and touched his arm. "I'm sorry. I didn't mean that to come out so . . . It's just that none of us know how to handle this. I'm so jumpy."

"That's all right. I feel the same way."

Together with Dan she walked him upstairs, though he could have found his own way. Perhaps she just needed to keep herself occupied. When she lingered at Jack's door, before he stepped in, Roy wondered whether she might be about to tell him something. But she just motioned him on.

"It's exactly as he left it," she said. "We haven't touched anything. Would you mind answering one question, Roy?"

"If I can."

"This doesn't have anything to do with that stupid game,

does it? I mean, he's been holed up in there for days, not showing his face, and I have to admit I was getting worried even before . . . y'know, before he went wherever he went. I mean, he's always *lived* for that computer, playing shoot-'em-ups till dawn and God knows what, but this time it was different, really different. The way he looked, Roy, I swear something was taking him over. He looked like a ghost the last time I saw him."

"I can only guess," Roy said. "I've played the game too, and there *is* more to it than I expected. It's very easy to get lost in Silicon Sphere."

"Lost? You mean literally lost?"

"I guess so. That hasn't happened to me, is all I can say. Maybe I didn't go into it as deeply as Jack or Kyle did, maybe I just got lucky . . ."

"I'd say you got lucky," Dan said abruptly. "The word is, the game's bad news. There are companies out there—companies like DataLite—who're even trying to outlaw the thing, though it's been loose on the Net for a while."

"But it's almost impossible to outlaw anything once it's loose on the Net," Roy said. "Just what is so bad about it?"

"I've heard rumors of kids who've suffered complete nervous breakdowns after playing it, and *I* sure wouldn't jump in, at least until I'd had a good look at the source code. All I know is, this is what people are saying. I know they used to say the same about movies and music—*this is poison, this is bad for your soul, and if you watch such and such you'll be corrupted forever*—but you only have to consider the side effects, the vanishings, the changes you're seeing right now in this town."

Roy considered. "I never felt in danger while playing it. It's certainly very real, but—"

"It's a drug, is what I told Jack," Sandy said. "It gets you hooked. But tell that to a junkie and the junkie will shrug and say, *Not me—no way!* And, believe me, Roy, as far as this game is concerned, Jack *was* a junkie. It took him right over." Sandy forced a smile, a bitter smile; her eyes were brimming. "I think we've kept you long enough. You know where everything is, anyway. I'll be downstairs if you want me."

"I won't be long."

Roy had watched Dan guide her away toward the stairs, then stepped into the room.

"And?" Alison Dougan said, raising her voice above the blare of car horns. The horns were meant for her; listening, rapt, to Roy's story, she had nearly crossed the center line, into the path of oncoming traffic. "And what did you find in there?"

"I'm telling you. The computer was on, for one thing. Sandy was right about nothing having been touched, because Jack had his computer fired up all of the time. There was a screen saver thing running, so I sat down and shifted the mouse to clear it and see what was on the screen.

"It was the desert—you know, on the way out past the

town in Silicon Sphere. It was just desert for miles and a storm whipping up across it, and the sky . . ." He broke off, frowning. "Well, the sky was pretty much the way it is now. I've never seen it like this before. Have you?"

Alison shook her head, no. She was slowing the Fiesta for a traffic light. "It's funny you saying that. It makes every thing look—"

"The same way it does in the game."

"That's what I was thinking. It's such an absurd idea."

"What idea?"

"That I brought a little piece of the Sphere home with me."

"You mean like this?" Roy said, brushing grains of sand from the dash into the palm of his hand. "I've thought the same thing from time to time. But in Jack's room, I really felt it. When I turned away from the desk, everything had a kind of airbrushed look. It seemed . . . pixillated, made up of millions of dots of color. It might've been the light in there, but I didn't think so at the time. I actually said to my-self, 'This isn't real. This goddamn place is an artist's impression of what some ordinary kid's room looks like.'"

Alison let out a low, appreciative whistle. "That's scary. Did the feeling pass?"

"No. In fact it grew on me. I got up and went to Jack's bookshelf. I wasn't looking for anything in particular, I just wanted to let everything wash over me. I thought that if I stayed awhile I might begin to see something, feel some-thing . . . which I did almost right away."

"You saw something? What?"

"No, I felt something. I can't really describe it, except that it felt like a presence. I was absolutely, one hundred percent sure there was someone else with me in the room. Even now, I'm certain they were there."

"Who?"

"I don't know. Maybe Jack."

"Did you hear him? Did he speak? Throw stuff around?"

"No, nothing like that. It was . . . how can I explain this? It was as if he was still there, exploring the Sphere, except that somehow there was more of him in the Sphere than in his room. He was there! Or *someone* was there. It had me thinking about vampire legends: the way the living dead cast no reflection in mirrors. Well, here was one better. There was someone in my space, casting no reflection in the room."

Alison drove in silence for a time, but it was clear her thoughts were racing. "Perhaps . . ." she murmured at last. "Perhaps . . . we should talk more to this boyfriend of Sandy's. Where does he work again?"

"Sandy said his company was called DataLite. There's a DataLite in the industrial park not far from here; they're owned by Vanguard."

"Shall we check them out?" Suddenly Alison sounded less weary, less ready for home than she had at first, as if the talk had fired her up. "Even if Dan isn't there, they can point us in the right direction, I'm sure."

"Are you sure? I mean, are you sure you want to take time out to do this?"

"Imagine we're still in the game," Alison said. "Let's explore a little deeper and see where it leads: you never know what's around the next corner. Hang onto your hat, Roy."

She floored the accelerator, whipping the Fiesta around the next corner.

IN THE SPHERE

CHAPTER SEVENTEEN

At first, Kate couldn't tell whether she'd woken from a dream or into one. Perhaps it was both.

Before she came to her senses, she could only see smoke, heavy and gray as fog: somewhere behind its dense cloak, intermittent flashes of dazzling yellow lit up the night.

They were setting off flares in the no-go zone. On every street, wherever she looked, gangs were overturning cars and torching buildings with homemade explosives. There were gunshots in the distance and a constant, chilling roar of voices. Above the fog, the sky was on fire.

It had come to this. Somewhere deep down, she'd always feared that it would, but never so soon. She'd been absent how long?—a day, maybe two at the most—and already the world had lost its grip. She hadn't wanted to return yet, at least not until she knew what had happened to Karin and Jack, but of all the luck she'd come round not in the Sphere but in the dark heart of the Riverside district.

A window box, crammed with dry, dead flowers, fell silently three floors out of blackness and exploded on the pavement six feet in front of her.

Kate jumped backward, startled, gasping.

No one saw her or cared. The mob were too preoccupied with larger matters, setting fire to the night, tearing down the ghetto into which the city had dumped them. Had the violence spread to other parts of Newton yet? Had it spilled beyond the police cordons to touch her family, her friends, the normal, sane world she remembered?

Sniper fire ricocheted off a wall to her right, spraying fragments of brick and cement across her vision, and she ducked quickly into an alley between two blackened buildings.

God help me, she thought. *Someone please help me . . .*

A figure moved slowly toward her out of the shadows: a tall, powerful figure of a man, the crown of his head gleaming as the light caught it. Behind him, twenty or thirty yards inside the alley, tongues of flame lapped brightly above a burning dumpster.

Kate felt her whole body grow tense, ready to run.

The figure, sensing what she had in mind, held up a hand. "Don't worry. I'm in control here."

"In control? Could anyone be in control of *this*?"

"You'd better believe it, honey."

"Who are you?"

"Call me Eddie. I'm your Maker. Or rather, I soon will be."

"That's all I need to hear," Kate said. "I'm outta here."

"No. Wait. I'm the only one you can depend on right now. Let me ask you a question. How would you rate your chances of making it out alive through that riot?"

"I'd say my chances are pretty slim either way. I'm not sure I'd be any safer with you than out there."

He edged forward again, still keeping his distance. As he did, the light of a blazing building on the street touched his face, and Kate stiffened. She couldn't be certain she had met this man before, but somehow she recognized him.

His eyes were hidden by tiny, round-lensed shades that mirrored the funeral pyre behind her; his lips formed a pinched, narrow smile. Suddenly he didn't strike her as dangerous so much as just plain bizarre. "What do you know about what's happening here?" she asked.

"Whatever you want to know."

"Is this for real, what I'm seeing?"

"That depends on your point of view. Here's the news: I'm for real, and so are you, but chances are, if one of those stray bullets strikes you, you'll wake up with a start."

Kate balked at that. "I'll wake up? I'm *dreaming* this?"

"You're dreaming about what might be, what will eventually be. And like all dreams, this is more than just a sensurround mind-movie: it's about your secrets and fears . . . the things you'd rather not think about. The difference is, this is *my* dream, too. I'm giving you a chance to see through my eyes. This is the way the world really is. It's what it's becoming. *Que sera sera.*"

Kate flinched as something behind her exploded with a muffled but deafening thud. The vibration felt like a fist in her gut. "Okay," she said to the figure called Eddie, "if this is my dream, and you're controlling whatever I see, then what's the point? Why do you *want* me to see this?"

"I'm offering you an alternative," he said. "A chance to improve your world, to stop it from becoming this monstrous thing."

"How? How can you do that?"

"I'll show you."

He snapped his fingers, and at once the walls of the alley capsized around her. Darkness rushed down, bringing rubble and fire.

Kate woke up shouting. Or perhaps she'd been shouting—or he, the man in the alley, had shouted—in her dream. Either way, her ears were ringing. She was still beaded with perspiration. But the dust was clearing from her sight, and the heat of burning buildings, the noise, the smell of scorched earth in her nostrils had become something else: cool and antiseptic.

Wait, just wait one damn minute, Kate thought. *If that vision of hell was the dream, than what's this?*

She was lying on some kind of solid surface, a table or bed, in a gray room. Ten or twelve feet above her, the ceiling was dotted with tiny, eye-sized spotlights. In fact, she realized as she tried flexing her limbs, she wasn't just resting here: she was being restrained by something that lay heavily across her chest and legs, straps perhaps, that she couldn't quite see from this angle. Straining, she managed to lift her head an inch or two above the pillow, far enough to feel something tug the skin at her temple. From somewhere behind her, out of the field of her vision, came the soft and steady bleep of a machine.

Jesus, what now?

A door opened across the room to her right. There were footsteps, and then the door closed with a metallic thud. Kate turned her face toward the sound in time to see the lower half of a girl walking toward her.

"Are you okay?" the visitor said, dragging a chair across the floor to the bedside. Her accent was foreign, perhaps north European.

"Where am I?" Kate asked.

"You're in Alphazone. Don't strain; I'm sitting down now. I'll explain."

Kate waited while the girl dropped onto the chair. She almost recognized her—but not quite. The thick tangle of auburn hair and piercing green eyes were so familiar she felt foolish that she couldn't put a name to the face. As if to complement the room itself, the girl was dressed all in gray, in a one-piece suit that could have been either a drab fashion statement or a uniform.

"I know you," Kate said. She was watching the girl intently. "*Do* I know you?"

"Of course. But this is the first time we've met."

"Then who—"

"Just a minute. Your straps are too tight. They really don't have a clue, do they? Anyone would think they're afraid you'll escape. Let me help."

175

The visitor leaned forward, loosening the ties one by one until Kate felt able to half sit up. She had to do so slowly, for the pressure at her temple increased and she felt a sudden wave of dizziness wash over her.

"Steady," the visitor said. "You'll hurt yourself if you're not careful."

"Go on," Kate said. "I know you. I *do* know you. But from where?"

"I'm Karin."

"Karin Mars?"

"The same. That's karin at nova dot com."

"Jesus, I don't believe this. Tell me I'm dreaming. No, no, I was dreaming just a minute ago. Tell me I've lost my mind and everything will be hunky-dory. At least I could deal with that."

"Sorry to disappoint you, K, but you're wide awake and doing just fine. They have to keep you monitored for a while, hence all these wires, but that's all in your best interests; they have to be sure."

"Sure of what?"

"Sure that it went as planned."

"I'm sorry." Kate was staring at her Net correspondent, nonplussed. "Either I'm not fully awake yet, or I left half my senses behind back there in the dream, but I don't understand a word you're saying. What went as planned, Karin? What went as planned?"

"The operation, of course."

At first Kate thought she must have misheard. But Karin

Mars's expression hadn't faltered; she was studying Kate with unblinking eyes.

Oh my God, Kate thought then, and whatever strength she still had seemed to drain from her body. *Oh my God, it just keeps getting worse* . . .

"It's all right, though," Karin said calmly, squeezing her hand. "I've been there already, and it's like a breath of fresh air, really it is. Out with the old data, in with the new. It's amazing what a difference a reformat can make, K. Just give it time, and I swear you'll never want to go back."

Chapter Eighteen

Like a rainbow crossing the sky after rain, the distant façade of Alphazone seemed to slip farther away the longer they drove toward it. For mile upon mile there had been only desert, red and barren as Martian terrain; then a weird silvery light had appeared, sandwiched between the horizon and the boiling clouds, and Janie had let out a shout that prickled Jack's nerves.

"That's it. Up ahead. I swear that's it."

The light was glinting even now, but it seemed hours since Janie had noticed it, and they were still no closer. Vern was at the Chevy's wheel, with Jack riding shotgun, Janie breathing down his neck and rocking back and forth nervously, and the others crammed in alongside her.

"Vern, what's happening?" Greg Sharp called from behind.

"Search me. A mirage?"

"Another trick," Janie said. "We've been duped into following the wrong highway."

"There's only one highway," Greg reminded her. "And we're on it. No, maybe something's brewing up ahead. Maybe they're expecting us."

"I'd still like to know who *they* are," Vern said.

Greg gave Hal a nudge. "Hey, Hal, who the hell *are* they? I never did ask you that."

Hal sat motionless as if in a trance, the silver light playing across his shades. Then he said simply, "The Fathers of the New Age and the next reality."

"I think we must've screwed up his ROMs back there," Greg said.

"Never mind, Hal," Janie said, and to the others, "Sounds to me like he's still stuck in boot mode. If that's the best he can do, I'd suggest reformatting from scratch, if that's possible."

"Something's happening all right." Vern, squinting, lifted a hand to shield his eyes as the light intensified. "I think the mirage is passing."

"He's right," Jack said. "We're closer now. *It's* closer. In fact—" He took another look, just to be sure. "In fact it's coming this way."

Some distance ahead, the light was forming itself into a shape, a solid mass rearing up out of the desert. At first it seemed to Jack that the clouds were regrouping themselves in the image of an outstretched hand, each clawlike finger perfectly defined. Then, as he blinked, the illusion shifted, and at once the shape had become something else: now the fingers were vague extremities, mutating into limbs, and the mass resembled that of a man striding forward in slow, giant steps across the red sand. The creature's eyes were blazing purple neon; bolts of lightning flickered across the vast chasm of its mouth. The flesh of its face and hands looked to Jack like pure molten metal.

179

"Jesus." Greg leaned forward from the back, gasping. "There must've been something in that coffee back there. Did you ever see anything like this?"

"Never," Jack said. "I think I can safely say you don't see this every day."

"So what now? What do we do now?" Vern demanded in a voice that sounded so shrill it might break into a howl any minute.

"Go with it, I guess." Jack swallowed hard. "Seems to me we don't have a hell of a lot of options."

"It may have escaped your notice," Vern said. "But we aren't exactly loaded to the hilt with AK47s and rocket launchers here. This is kind of all new to me. I mean, I'm not sure we're equipped to *deal* with this situation. This ain't another Warzone shoot-'em-up, Jack."

"Exactly. There's more going on here than we understand, a lot of phony thrills and distractions, but I haven't seen a single drop of blood spilled yet."

"What about those guards Hal blew away in the elevator?" Greg asked.

"Hell, they weren't even *human,* were they? They were machines; half-breeds like Hal at the very least. Did you see them bleed when Hal shot them?"

Janie sounded convinced. "He has a point. This place is just one big wall-to-wall mind game. Someone's toying with us, trying to throw us off the scent."

"So what do I do?" Vern practically hollered. "While

you're discussing this over coffee and cakes, *I'm* driving toward that thing."

"Just keep driving," Jack said. It was a hunch, but to re-
treat now would accomplish nothing; it would send them
right back to where they began—Do Not Pass Go—and Kate
would be further out of reach than ever.

"Do I have a consensus on that?" Vern said.

"Yeah. Drive," Greg said.

"Damn right," Janie said. "Drive straight at that sucker.
Slaughter the dragon, save the fair maiden. Burn rubber,
baby!"

"Where did you say you went to finishing school?" Vern
asked, flooring the accelerator.

The creature rose up to full height as they approached.
Flashes of lightning played at the tips of its outstretched fingers; thunder rocked the ground as it took one more giant
pace forward. The Chevy couldn't have been more than
four or five hundred yards short of the beast when its fea-
tures began to mutate again.

In the back seat, Janie took in a short, sharp gasp of air;
Greg clutched the rim of the seat in front of him.

"You want me to keep on going?" Vern said. "Because, if
you dudes are really not sure, I'd be only too happy to swing
this thing around—"

"You bet," Greg told him. "You bet. Keep your foot
down, Vern."

"Are you out of your mind? If I—"

181

"What the hell is it doing now?" Janie said.

It was hard to distinguish exactly, if only because the creature's flesh had begun to melt. Its hands and face were transforming, almost at random; liquid chrome snakes squirmed up from its head like jewels in a gorgon's crown. The eyes were still flames of neon, but the cavernous mouth was agape, and something—Jack hardly dared look—was emerging from inside it.

"Oh, *gross.*" Janie sounded properly disgusted. "Cyber-vomit or what? What is this?"

There was no time to answer her question. They had driven into the heart of the creature, and suddenly the substance escaping the demon's mouth was striking the car on all sides, hammering the windshield so hard there was nothing to see until Vern switched on the wipers.

"It's hail," Jack said quickly. His heart was pounding; he was terrified but wildly exhilarated, exactly the way he'd always felt in Zone Eleven. "The storm's here. We're right in the middle of it."

"Where did it go?" Vern wanted to know. "I mean, where did that fifty-foot psycho go? It was here just a second ago?"

"That psycho," Jack said, "*was* the storm."

The hail was coming so hard he could barely hear himself speak or think. Janie cried out as the window on her side cracked, struck by a ball of hail the size of a fist. The windshield, too, was suffering damage; a spider's web of splin-

182

tered glass spun out inches from Jack's face, doubling and tripling its size as another hailstone struck, then another.

Suddenly there was no more desert. The storm, the avalanche of hail, had blotted it out as far as the eye could see—only fifteen or twenty feet on all sides at most. Vern had dropped the Chevy's speed to walking pace and was doubling himself forward across the wheel, frowning to see what lay ahead.

"Go faster," Greg yelled.

"You're kidding. I can't see a goddamn thing."

"Go faster. The faster we go, the sooner we'll be out of this thing."

"Hell, what should I know? I'm just the driver."

Vern stabbed the accelerator. Thunder sounded, seemingly only a few feet from the car, or perhaps that was the sound of the hail, thrashing the ground so hard it was causing the Chevy to shudder.

"Hold on, hold on," Vern said. "Something's happening here . . ."

It was still impossible to see more than a few feet ahead, but now Jack imagined—perhaps it was just wishful thinking—that the onslaught was fading and a silvery light lay across the horizon again. As Vern drove, the wipers going full tilt, the hail imperceptibly dissolved into rain, and beyond the rain lay more boiling clouds; and beyond the clouds light, and—

"Alphazone," Janie yelled, clutching Jack's shoulder. She

must have sensed it, for it seemed to Jack that minutes passed before he could make it out for himself.

But Janie was right; in spite of the pounding rain, rain so heavy the desert sands beyond the windshield were swirling like mud, there were signs of the complex, the source of the silver light.

"Home sweet home," Hal said quietly.

This time, there was no illusion. This wasn't a wavering, soft-wedged mirage like before. The grouping of square buildings—the flat, cell-like boxes Janie and Greg had described—were aglow, and at last it was possible to pinpoint the source of the light.

"You were right," Jack said. "It looks like . . . Jesus, like a *brain,* for crying out loud."

His gaze was fixed on the dome at the heart of the complex. It towered above Alphazone like a sentinel, radiating light from its huge, metal crown. Fingers of lightning crisscrossed the sky above it, reflecting themselves in its mirrored surface. It was only as Vern slammed on the Chevy's brakes at the perimeter fence that Jack saw something else: the dome, the brain, whatever the hell it was, appeared to be moving, pulsating, as if currents of blood, or strange, troubled dreams, were being pumped through it.

"Welcome to Alphazone," Vern said, getting out. "Did you guys enjoy the ride?"

"Where do we go from here?" Jack asked. He was staring, mesmerized, at the dome.

"As far as I can remember, we're not far from that gap in

the fence," Greg said. "We should still be able to get through there."

"What about Hal?"

"What *about* Hal?"

"Does he stay here or come with us?"

Greg considered this. "I guess Hal is with us. He may not be much use as he is right now, but he's one of them; he might just be our ticket inside."

The rain was letting up at last. Beyond the perimeter fence, the Alphazone courtyard was waterlogged and deserted. In spite of appearances—the site seemed completely empty— Jack couldn't help feeling under observation as he followed the others toward the main building. Greg led the way, guiding Hal gently forward by the arm; Hal stumbled forward, as if his body and what remained of his mind were unsynchronized; Janie and Vern followed two steps behind. From here, directly below the dome and its pulsing brain, Jack suddenly felt very small, as if in some way he had always belonged to the game, to Silicon Sphere, not as a player but as another of its many super-realistic details. Here he was no more significant, no more important than the clouds overhead, the swirling sheets of desert sand, the morphing Marilyn billboard back in the town.

And maybe, he thought with a shudder, *I'm not more real than anything else here, either. Maybe I'm just something someone dreamed up one day, someone who really doesn't give a good damn whether I survive or cease to exist. . . .*

"In here," Greg said, breaking Jack's reverie. "This is where the guards took me before."

They had come to a halt in front of an outbuilding, three stories high, its walls as anonymous and gray as those Jack remembered from the Riverside quarter. The many small barred windows, Jack saw, were darkened but somehow alive, as if each concealed a face staring out. He sensed a thousand eyes boring into him, even though there was no sign of life.

"Are you up for this, Hal?" Greg asked. "Do you remember why you're here?"

Hal nodded.

"More importantly," Janie said, "do you remember why you defected? Why you joined us?"

"Malfunction," Hal replied. "System trap; error code 1939."

"Well, that's pretty coherent at least." Janie rolled her eyes heavenward. "Thanks for clearing that up for me."

"It'll be just like before, Hal," Greg said. "Except this time you're with us, not them. You'll lead us inside as if you've taken us captive, okay? And you'll take us to the cells where the prisoners are kept. Have you got that?"

"Got it. Data assimilated. Rechecking instruction set. Ready."

Greg looked at the others. "You ready too?"

"For all it's worth," Vern said, shrugging, lifting his hands.

Jack nodded. "Me, too."

Together, they started into the foyer.

186

The atmosphere inside was claustrophobic: gray metal walls enclosed them, shining dully beneath a cast of dimmed ceiling spots. There was no one in sight, but the distant hum of machinery somewhere in the building hinted that Alphazone wasn't as vacant as it seemed. A bank of four elevators lay straight ahead, three of the doors standing wide open, the fourth secretively closed. The wall panels inside were chrome, reflecting dim light from the foyer.

"So far so good," Greg said. "Which floor, Hal?"

"First floor for Research and Development, Programming and Reformatting; second floor for Post-op and Reconstruction."

"Jesus God." Jack could scarcely contain himself. "Did he just say Post-op and Reconstruction? It's worse than I thought."

Greg Sharp was guiding him into the elevator. "The question is, which stage is your friend at? If she's lucky, she won't have gone as far as reformatting yet. Let's check the first floor."

Dry-mouthed, Jack watched the elevator doors hiss shut, and the floor-indicator light click up one notch. The others bunched at the doorway, watching the floor, hardly breathing. There were five or six seconds of absolute silence. Then, as the elevator settled, Greg Sharp looked up and directly at Jack.

"Okay?"

"Yeah, I'm ready."

The doors opened. Ahead was a pale gray corridor, its

walls lined by high-tensile steel doors. Greg had described it accurately. There was a distant, mute rumbling, perhaps a tremor of thunder outside or an echo down below in the elevator shaft. For a moment Jack felt frozen to the spot, unable to move from the rear wall of the elevator. He watched, unmoving, while the others piled out.

Where are your nerves of steel? he chastised himself. *What happened to the king of hyperspace? Some king you are. Some time this is to lose your edge. . . .*

"Jack?" Janie said.

"I'm okay. I'm coming."

There wasn't much further to go, anyhow. They had entered the demon's stronghold; now all that remained was to slaughter the dragon and save the fair maiden. No sweat. Jack almost laughed aloud at the thought: this particular quest was nowhere near over; in a way, it had barely begun.

As he stepped into the corridor he heard the distant rumble again: thunder, definitely . . . maybe. He hesitated at the elevator door, sensing a sudden change in the atmosphere, a drop in the temperature, his sixth sense ticking nervously. Jack knew this feeling well; it was exactly the way he always felt out in Zone Eleven, seconds before the battle cruisers showed up on his vessel's radar. Something was coming. It was very nearly close enough to touch. A look of confusion and maybe fear passed across Janie's face like a cloud. There was silence again, a fragile stillness, and then Hal was launching himself at a wall away to Jack's left.

"Hal—whaddya doing? What the hell are you—"

Greg threw himself forward, but too late to prevent Hal from landing his full weight on a polished red lever that hung from the wall like a tongue. It must have been some kind of panic button, because already the alarm was sounding inside Jack's head.

"Attention!" Hal was yelling at the top of his lungs. "Attention! New arrivals! Attention!"

"He bluffed us!" Janie was mouthing above the noise. "He double-bluffed us! That no good android sonofabitch—"

"Back the way we came," Greg hollered, but the elevator doors were already sealing themselves up again, and halfway along the corridor something was beginning to emerge from the walls.

Jack realized almost at once what was happening. The gray metal walls were suddenly malleable and soft, and recognizable shapes—faces, hands, torsos—were forming, as if pushing themselves through from the other side. They came like snakes, squirming and reaching. Somewhere behind him, Jack heard Janie let out a sigh of disgust. Suddenly the place was crawling with half-complete creatures—no, more than that: humanoid forms, guards, faces still indistinct, molten-metal hands clutching weapons, their flesh gleaming like chrome. *They say walls have ears,* Jack thought, *but this is ridiculous.*

"Man, why don't they come through the doors like other people?" Vern wanted to know. There was panic in Vern's voice—a panic Jack felt deep down in himself, in the others too—as he grabbed at the closed elevator doors, beating the gleaming panels with both fists.

"Hal, if I ever see you again, you are *toast*," Greg said, and then a fully formed guard knocked him to the floor with the butt of his rifle.

Greg rolled over, lay still.

Somewhere, Janie was screaming.

The guard swung around toward Jack, rifle still at a tilt. His face had a silvery sheen; more moonlight on metal than flesh. Mirror-lensed shades concealed his eyes, making his face unreadable. As two of his cohorts grabbed Jack from behind, however, he began to smile.

"What's to smile about?" Jack was furious, kicking and thrashing, though his arms were clamped tight. "You think this is goddamn funny?"

"I'm not amused," the guard said. "Just surprised. To see you, that is."

"You're *what?*"

"I'm sorry it has to be this way. Years from now you'll look back and you'll know why it had to be: it'll all make sense. Jack, we *were* made for this. It's true, believe me," Kyle said, removing his shades.

CHAPTER NINETEEN

He dreamed strange dreams for a while, monochrome dreams of city streets bustling with empty-eyed, straight-faced clones; then he woke slowly, uncomfortably, on gray nylon sheets on a bunk in a cool echoing cell. His head spun uncertainly; nerves flinched behind his eyes as if the migraines he'd suffered after playing Silicon Sphere for the first time were about to return. Though the ceiling spots were dimmed, their light cast garish patterns across the steel walls. Across the room, a blurred face watched him through what seemed like a sheet of beveled glass. The eyes of the face appeared like dark empty sockets, the eyes of a living skull.

Then the room became dark and Jack slept again.

Some time later, the scuffing of feet across the tiled floor brought him around. So he wasn't alone—the guards had dumped Janie and Greg and Vern in here too; they reclined, asleep, on bunks along the opposite wall—but he might as well have been alone. What he'd dreamed had only made him feel worse. He felt abandoned and clueless, at a loss for ideas. They would never get out of this place alive, he was sure. It was one thing to crash to your death in a flight sim, but this particular defeat felt final. Kyle was the master of cyber-reality, and if Kyle had succumbed, what chance did anyone else have? Kyle's, as far as he could tell, had been the last face he'd seen before the need to sleep overcame him.

Jack closed his eyes and drifted.

The pattern of sleeping, waking, and sleeping continued, until voices forced him once more to his senses, and he managed to force himself upright in bed.

"But do you feel any different?" Vern was saying.

"I can't say so. I can't say I feel anything at all right now," Janie said.

"I've got pictures in my head," Greg Sharp said, sounding more entranced than concerned. "It's like, I'm dreaming but I'm still wide awake. I can picture where we are and how here relates to everywhere else. I can see right across the desert to the town. I've got a map of this place in my head, you guys. I could draw it for you right now."

"All *I* can see is ones and zeros," Vern said.

"I'm afraid," Janie said. "Something's happened to us. What did they do, Greg? What did they do to us?"

"I don't know, but it doesn't feel all bad. I'm not hurting. Are you?"

"Is this what being reformatted feels like?" Jack asked. His tongue felt slow and Novocaine-numb.

"Jack, you're awake." Janie gave him the most reassuring smile she could manage; not very. She looked tense and pale.

"Well, this isn't what I expected," Vern said. "I still know

192

who I am, and I know who you all are. I sure haven't wound up like Hal, thank God. This feels like someone just flushed the cobwebs out of my brain, but *that* dude must've undergone a full-blown personality bypass."

"Who was the kid with the rifle?" Greg asked. "You seemed to know him."

"That was Kyle," Jack said. "He's a friend. *Was* a friend. A friend of Roy McKee's."

"*That* Roy? The guy I e-mail all the time? Jeez, you all know each other? You never told me that."

"Somehow I never got around to it. It was Roy that downloaded Silicon Sphere from the Net, and we all took copies. A friend of yours, Bill Wallis, posted it to him from Northwestern."

Greg shook his head, marveling. "Small virtual world, pal. Small virtual world." Then he gave his shoulder an exaggerated rub where the rifle butt had struck him. "I can't say I'm crazy about your friend Kyle, though."

"That's what I can't understand. Kyle would have—should have—been with us, not against us. Kyle was always a winner; when it came to computers he hated to lose even at chess. He lived and breathed this stuff. Couldn't get enough of it. He's the one I would've thought would show up at the last minute to haul us out of this mess. And now look . . ."

"I don't get it," Janie said. "I just don't get it."

"Maybe we're missing something," Greg said.

"Like what, for instance?"

193

"Like maybe Kyle didn't fail; maybe the Forces of Darkness didn't beat him into submission. Maybe he joined them willingly."

"Meaning what?"

"I don't know. Suppose he *likes* it here—suppose he knows something we don't, or maybe he just saw enough to decide he wanted to make a go of it."

"No. No, that's impossible."

"Is it? Then answer me this: why did *you* keep coming back, Jack?"

Jack was almost at a loss to explain; it seemed so long since his first visit here that he'd almost forgotten how it felt. "To beat it, I suppose. To solve the mystery, figure it all out. Isn't that why we're all here?"

"No. It's why you all think you're here."

Jack did a double take, initially wondering how Greg had managed to say that without moving his lips; but the voice came from across the room to his right. A tall man dressed head to foot in black stood at the doorway, his lips pursed in a thin smile, his bald scalp gleaming. The narrow cheeks and dark clothing gave him an ominous, almost ghostly appearance. His collarless jacket was buttoned to the throat; his eyes were hidden by the obligatory tiny, round-lensed shades. From where Jack was seated the man looked something like Hal; in fact he looked uncomfortably like Hal—a virtual doppelgänger.

"Welcome to Alphazone," the man in black said. "The name is Matrix. Now why don't we all step into my office?"

■   ■   ■

The office in question was a short distance away. Having dispersed the guards, Matrix led the way across the courtyard to the building beneath the dome. An elevator carried them to the top, where the panoramic view took Jack's breath away. From the windows in Matrix's office you could see the edge of the world—or at least the graphically rendered, virtual world. Desert stretched out for miles beneath a canopy of swirling red storm. Lights in the town and from other, unexplored towns farther away glimmered in the distance.

Now here, Jack thought, *is the center of it all, the heart of the Sphere, or rather its brain, and a pretty disturbed brain at that.* The room seemed somehow alive, as though a constant, electric undercurrent pulsed throughout it.

"You must feel like God up here," Vern remarked.

Matrix shot him a look. "Yes, as a matter of fact I do."

"So who are you?" Greg said.

"Call me, Eddie."

"You're—you're in charge here?"

"All this belongs to me, if that's what you mean."

"What happened to the others?" Jack wanted to know. "Kate and . . . Karin . . . and all the others on the news reports? Are they like Kyle? Like Hal? What did you *do* to them?"

"Just a moment. It'll all become clear soon enough."

Matrix stooped over his desk, flicked an intercom switch. "Send her in now," he said.

Almost at once, the outer door to Matrix's office buzzed

open. A girl stood at the threshold, dressed in what was beginning to seem to Jack like a uniform; the gray plastic uniform worn by new recruits in Alphazone, the ones who had been reprogrammed.

It was Kate.

"I think you two know each other," Matrix said, turning to Jack. "As you can see, she's in good health. Ask her yourself if you don't believe me."

Jack took a step forward. The whole room seemed to waver unsteadily about him as Kate's eyes met his: Kate was smiling, but there was something missing, a spark that had set him alight one morning not so long ago as she smiled at him during the bus ride to school.

"Kate? Are you—"

"Yes, Jack, I'm . . . well. Never better."

"You know me?"

"Of course I do."

"Do you remember? Do you remember how you got here?"

"Yes. I remember . . . *everything.*"

Jack cast a nervous look at the others. Kate's demeanor, her tone, unsettled him; she sounded aloof and distant. "But you're not the same; something happened to you, Kate. They did something to you. *Matrix* did something to you."

"Yes, to all of us. Don't imagine you're so very different, Jack."

Jack felt a wave of pure coldness pass through him. He

didn't want to have to accept this, he was trying to close his mind to the obvious, but it was now unavoidable. Once you entered the Sphere, you were changed forever, in every way. Perhaps he had known that all along, but only now did he realize how deeply those changes were rooted. For all he knew, there could be a time bomb inside his head. And Kate was with Matrix now; she belonged to the Sphere. He looked at Matrix, aghast. "Exactly what kind of demented regime are you running here? You treat us like prisoners, put us through surgery—"

"Let's not forget you came here by choice."

"Sure," Janie said, "at least to begin with, but we didn't know then what we know now. I mean, I don't recall being asked if I actually *wanted* to be reformatted. We thought— we thought this was just infotainment."

"Really? But I'd say you wanted much more than that. You wanted to reach new heights in game-playing. You wanted to go places you'd never been before, take part in the newest, coolest thing, and you would've given anything for it. I've given you what you desired: the complete VR experience."

"You're crazy," Jack said.

"Maybe so. Or maybe I'm very sane indeed."

"So what is it you want? Why are you doing this?"

A cloud shifted across the lenses of Matrix's shades. "I need a captive audience. I need messengers to go out from here, spread this vision of mine across the world. When you've heard me out, you can make up your own minds. The fact of the matter is, I offer you only one thing: a new beginning. I'm building something new, and you can be part of it, if you want to be."

Janie was fingering her temple. "Do we really have a choice?"

"You can stay or go," Kate said, edging past Matrix's desk to the window, where she stood with her back to the storm. "I've already made that decision, and I chose to stay. Think about it, why don't you? Imagine what you'll really be leaving behind. It took me a little while before I saw the light, but then everything here seemed to make total sense. There's no going back to the old world now."

"But that's *your* world," Janie said. "You can't just run away from it."

"Can't I? Well, I can, and I have. *This* is my world now. Just tell me, if you're all so connected to life back home, why did you keep coming here to escape it? Why didn't you just get on with your lives and forget this place? Why couldn't you quit?"

Jack was shaking his head, though. "Kate, do you really know what you're saying? You'd rather have this—the desert, the empty streets, the man-machines, the storms that never end—than your home?"

"*This* is my home, Jack. I've been waiting all my life for something like this. If you could just see what I've seen—"

"It won't always be like this," Matrix said. "The storms will pass. All that stands before you, the miles of desert, will flourish in time. First we have to populate the place, recruit new residents, and we'll build from there. Jack, I kid you not, my dream has become a reality. Soon the Sphere will be unrecognizable. It's growing even as we speak."

"You'd let us go? Just like that?"

"You have the same choice that Kate has. You're carrying a new chip, the same model of chip as hers, inside you, but that isn't there to remote-control you; it supplements the human brain, not replaces it. It's my gift to you."

"And for what?"

"It's there to serve you. You can store all the information you'll ever need right there. You want to read *War and Peace* in one night? Or read all the great books in your midterm break? Go ahead. You want to create a great work of art? If you can dream it, you can do it. Prefer to watch a movie without staring at a screen in the dark? Check it out. We're all so info-hungry these days, but we've never been able to take it all in. Now we can. It's my gift to you, Jack, a little piece of the Sphere to take home. If you don't like it come back and we'll refund your money, no questions asked."

"This is madness," Greg muttered.

"Is it? Are you certain of that?"

Matrix stepped aside so that Jack and the others had a clear view through the great window beyond the desk. At first, Jack could see little that he hadn't already seen. Outside, the red storm brooded; lightning sparkled across the desert, clouds patrolled the sky all the way from Alphazone to infinity. But slowly, very gradually, there was change.

There was sunlight somewhere beyond the clouds, and the clouds were parting like curtains, shrinking away from a deeper, clearer blue sky than Jack had ever seen in his life. As they did, the landscape itself seemed to transform itself. For an instant Jack had an uninterrupted view of silver waves washing along empty shorelines, than climbing to dizzy heights before crashing over the land. Some distance out to sea, perhaps half a mile from the coast, the crippled husk of a tanker floated, half submerged in the blackness. The oil it was spilling was on fire. Black poisonous clouds spewed upward, blotting out the last of the light.

Then the scene changed to a city, a nameless, dull brown city torn apart by the elements. Could this be Newton? The bombed-out highrises reminded Jack strongly of Riverside. The vacuum of a great tornado skipped across its suburbs, ripping up rooftops, casting them aside, imploding walls as if they were made of cardboard. It could have been Jack's imagination, but, even as he watched, the tornado had begun to resemble a mushroom cloud, the last word in manmade horrors, boiling above the city, filling the sky. In a matter of seconds the buildings were scorched white, gone, history.

"The end is beginning," Matrix said calmly, as if narrating some doomsday documentary. "It's time to wipe the slate clean, time to replace the old with the new. Long live the Virtual State! Soon you'll be unable to tell the difference between the world you left behind and what you see right here in the Sphere; and in time, *this* will be all there is. The old world and the new will become one."

"It's happening already," Kate said, her voice deadpan and cold. "Remember how Newton looked the last time you saw it, Jack? Remember the ray-traced buildings?"

Trapped in the window's frame, whole streets and suburbs were turned bright red, then white, then slowly dissolving into something new. Vast iron bridges liquefied into lakes of hot metal. Then, as they watched, the metal cooled, and great tower blocks with mirrored walls shimmered like molten chrome, reflecting the clouds that crossed the purple-blue sky.

"Never underestimate the wilderness," Matrix went on. "Never believe that nothing can thrive there. To some of you Las Vegas might seem like hell on earth, but to me it was always an inspiration. I mean, someone *dreamed that up*; incredibly, someone actually brought that all together in the middle of nowhere. To achieve such a thing, you must be a visionary, or completely insane, maybe both.

"And one day I found myself in the desert too, not far from Vegas. I was staying at some cheap motel off the highway, and I had nothing in the world at that time apart from my name, the data inside my head, and a length of jack cable. It's a long story, how I got to be there and the condition I was in by the time I arrived, but in short I settled back on the bed, plugged myself into the phone line and began to dream."

"Dream what?" Greg asked in a quiet, very subdued voice.

"All that you see before you. I dreamed of a new start, a place where I could begin again. And everything that was on my mind at the time—I just let it all out, all my memories, my thoughts, everything, and my thoughts became flesh. It was a primal scream, except that this scream was silent and came from somewhere in here." Matrix lifted a hand to his forehead. "To begin with, I thought I was dying. My mind was riddled with viruses, but the scum who put them there had underestimated me. I knew I was unique, the first of a new breed. I had the emotions of a man and the power of Vanguard Systems' latest and greatest processor chip on my side.

"There were vast information databases in here, in my head, but by the time I was able to compile the program data I needed, trace the viral strains and assimilate them, the bugs in me were already transforming . . . everything. You've witnessed the first changes already. All that you see has grown out of me. The world inside my mind has become solid and real, or at least as solid and real as any data can be. And the dream became Silicon Sphere, which you drooled about and downloaded to your desktops. And each time you entered the game, every time you played, you punched a small hole in the space between here and there, and a little more of this dream escaped into yours. You believed you were tapping into hot pirated software, but you were in fact tapping into me."

Jack flashed a glance at the others. They all looked equally awestruck; all except Kate, who seemed to be equal to the news. Then again, she'd had longer to take it all in.

"You . . . you're saying we're inside your head?" Janie said, her voice rising from a murmur to a shout. "We're inside your goddamn *head*?"

"Not physically inside my head—but you're in my thoughts and my thoughts are incarnate now, all around me. Everything here belongs to me. The streets in the town you've passed through are from photographs my folks brought home from their trip to Spain, the billboards and signs are a nod to Vegas. Remember Natasha at Paolo's coffee shop? She was my first love; a computer creation that broke my heart. And because I remember her so, I gave life to her, here. And Hal—"

"Well, Hal is one foul-up if ever I saw one," Greg said quickly.

"He has problems, I'll give you that. His nanochip needs upgrading. Until I get around to that, he'll remain as flaky as ever. But Hal is a memory of myself, before I overcame what Vanguard did to me."

"Vanguard?" Jack said. "I know someone who works for them. *They* did this to you?"

"Close enough. Vanguard didn't. Leon Speakes, the low life who runs Vanguard, did."

"Is this something to do with revenge, then? Are you planning an outright war against him?"

"The next war will be digital. We're already moving away from bombs and poison gas to data crimes, but I don't really want any part of that, except where Speakes is concerned. He stole from me, he took something precious, something I'd been working toward for years. The Vanguard OS is my own creation."

"*You* wrote that?" Greg Sharp gasped.

Matrix nodded. "And he made me into this thing you see standing before you. He very nearly destroyed me. But his time will come: I imagine that very soon now, Vanguard will come crashing down, and the truth will come out."

Suddenly, for the first time, Jack felt a rush of sympathy for the crazy man; or perhaps he wasn't so crazy after all. He was a victim as much as a villain.

"How will you ever get even with Speakes?" Vern asked. "That hotshot is bigger than God *and* Bill Gates. He's practically running the infobahn single-handed these days. He's remodelled Fort Knox around himself."

"Sure," Matrix said. "But the word is that Speakes will take the nanochip implant himself very soon. It's only a matter of time before he does. There's no reason why he shouldn't feel safe with me out of the way, and the lure of the New is too much to resist, we all know that. But . . . and here's the deal . . . even from here I can still hack into Vanguard's system. In here—" Matrix tapped his right temple with a forefinger—"I already have a series of high-resolution scans of Leon Speakes' brain patterns and a direct link to the sonofabitch's laptop. You can imagine the rest, I'm sure. The first time he hooks himself up to the wire, I'll have him. And when that moment comes, he's going to face more than a simple reformat. No, this will be a far greater thing. I'm talking about erasure. A low-level format with no new information to wipe out the old. The dude will become a blank, with just enough left in his head to know what he's lost."

Jack looked at Matrix, then at the others. He felt caught between horror and sheer admiration. "I'd say that would make you even."

"More than even," Matrix said. "But first, I want to see the empire crumble. That's where you come in."

"What do you want, exactly?"

"I'm asking no special favors of you. Just go back to where you came from, plug yourselves in, log on, and start telling my story. Upload your thoughts, for crying out loud. You have very special abilities now, so use them; do what you have to do. The chips you're carrying contain the whole story. The rest you can leave to me."

Jack looked at the others, at their astonished expressions. Janie was moving her lips wordlessly, mouthing sentiments she couldn't express. This was the end of the line, then. There was a way out, but Matrix had needed to tell his story before pointing the way to it.

"That's right," Kate said in a low voice, almost a whisper. She came forward, gave Jack a quick hug. "You're free to go. You can do whatever you want now."

"And you?"

"What do you think?"

205

"Reading you loud and clear. You choose to stay."

Kate shrugged. "Maybe I'll come home once in a while, just for a visit. Maybe I'll see you then."

"And maybe I'll see you here. Who knows?" Jack said. Right now he didn't know what he wanted; perhaps, in time, he'd decide.

Kyle was waiting outside. He was grinning as usual; he'd always looked this way every time after locking into a new game, Jack thought. "I'm going to escort you out of here," Kyle announced. "You're seriously telling me you don't want any part of this? You want to go back?"

"I'm not telling you anything yet," Jack said. "You probably haven't seen the last of me, Kyle."

"Glad to hear it."

"This place has a long way to go yet," Kate said as they strolled to the perimeter. "But it has possibilities, you have to admit that, and Matrix really is a believer. I think we have a real chance of building something here. Soon all our memories and ideas will start growing; we'll fill all those empty houses and cafés. You'll have to book a room in advance at the hotel the next time you come, Jack. There will be a next time, won't there?"

He kissed her lightly on the cheek as they reached the perimeter fence, then stood for a long moment to take in the view. As if to enhance his feeling that the mystery had finally unraveled itself, the clouds were giving way to sun across the desert. A light-headed, ozone-washed sense of relief swept over him. Just beyond the fence, the Chevy stood, dripping dry in the storm's afterglow.

"No hard feelings?" Kyle said to Greg Sharp. "About earlier, I mean. I always had a head for role-playing games; I just never really knew where to draw the line, is all."

"Lucky you caught me on a good day, then," said Greg. "But next time, bud, watch *out*."

Kyle laughed. Then he swept a bundle of keys from his pocket. "See here, Jack? I had these cut at Stan's auto in Newton. My very own set. God, I love that car. It's a wreck, but I love it." He gave Jack a firm slap between the shoulder blades, rolling Jack three paces forward. "Okay, if you're ready, I'll drive you back."

"I never thought to ask about that," Jack said. "How *do* we get out."

"You'll be fine," Kyle said. "Matrix doesn't need to keep you now he's spoken his piece. I'll drop you on the main street, you know where all the all-singing billboards are? Then retrace your steps from there. Oh, and I've also sent out e-mail for all of you, so wherever you're going there should be someone to meet you when you get back."

"Take it easy," Kate called from beyond the fence as they reached the car. "Come see us again any time."

"I love this place, dudes," Vern marveled, shaking his head. "I'm coming back here soon, I swear to God, I'm coming again with my freakin' bags packed."

"Shut up and move over," Janie told him. "There's hardly enough room back here for us *and* your mouth."

207

Jack turned to watch through the rear window while Kyle swung the Chevy around, nosing it back toward town. Kate waved vigorously for a time, then dropped her hands to her sides, staring after them. By the time the journey had reduced her to a speck in the distance, Jack was beginning to wonder whether he'd made the right choice after all.

Chapter Twenty

"Dan Morrisey? It's Alison Dougan. I'm in your office. Your secretary said it would be okay to call you from here. Where are you?"

"In my car. I'm on my mobile. Alison *who* did you say?"

"Dougan. Alison Dougan. I'm here with a friend of Jack North's. Roy McKee. You know him?"

"Yeah. I met him at Jack's, didn't I?"

"That's right. We need to talk to you about Jack . . . and about Silicon Sphere."

There was silence on the line for a time. Then Dan said, "In that case you're in the wrong place. Meet me at Jack's house instead. I'm on my way there right now. I'll explain when I see you."

"Well, what did he say?" Roy asked as she replaced the receiver.

"Not very much, but he sounded excited. Better get moving."

There were too many vehicles on the street for Alison to park close to the house. Leaving the Fiesta around the corner, they walked to Jack's, past a police car and a van from the BBC, among others. Roy saw a black BMW, abandoned, slanting across the curb as if its driver had been in a race of some kind.

"Well, *something's* happening," Roy said. "Someone's been drumming up publicity, but for what?"

"I guess we'll soon know. I hope this group all have their parking permits."

The door was already open at Jack's, probably because the house could contain no more visitors. The hall was crammed and noisy; camera flashlights were going off; everyone was talking at once. A couple of freelance reporters whom Roy had seen locally stood scribbling feverishly in their notebooks. Jack's mother and father wavered in the doorway to the living room, exhausted and pale. For a moment Roy feared that Jack's mother was fainting; guiding her away, into the living room, her husband closed the door after them.

"Roy!" someone called through the crowd.

At first he couldn't see where the voice was coming from. There were too many bodies blotting out the light, and the noise made it impossible to tell where the voice came from. Then he saw a hand waving above the sea, and a face fell into focus: Sandy. She was waving him over.

"There," Roy said, giving Alison a nudge.

"Upstairs," Sandy gestured, mouthing the words. "Come upstairs."

Two police were posted like sentries at the foot of the stairs, but once Sandy had pointed out Roy and Alison, the police stood aside to let them pass.

"I think Jack's coming," Sandy said breathlessly when Roy had caught up with her at the top. "Some welcome-home party, isn't it?"

"What's happening?" Alison asked.

"Ask Dan; he seems to have some idea. I'll take you to him."

"Why all the people?"

"I think one reporter started it all. He's a friend of Dan's, but he has a big mouth, and I imagine he's been spreading the rumor. He could've had his hands on a world exclusive, too, the big dummy."

"What's that I can hear?" Roy said, straining to filter out the hubbub downstairs. The sound of white noise, or something very much like it, seemed to be rising from somewhere near by.

"Along here. You'll find out soon enough. Dan? *Dan*?"

She led the way along the landing to Jack's room. The door opened just as they reached it, and Dan Morrisey stepped out, taking in Alison and Roy with one nervous glance. He was trying to smile but couldn't quite make it; the muscles of his face were drawn tight. "Hi, Roy. This thing just keeps on getting weirder, doesn't it? We spoke on the phone just now, didn't we?" he said, turning to Alison.

"That's right." A tremor had crept into her voice. "Can you explain what's going on here?"

"Something incredible, I think. Something I *can't* explain, not yet anyway." Behind him, the rush of white noise seemed to be growing. "Jesus, I've seen some things in my time, but this is all new. Here's the story: about an hour ago I got an e-mail from someone called Kyle Hallaway. You know Kyle?"

Roy and Alison looked at each other, wide-eyed.

"Sandy told me you would. The sender address was pretty much like any other Net address: kyle at alphazone, or something or other. Does that mean anything to you?"

"You bet," Roy said excitedly. "Go ahead. What did he say?"

"Just this: 'Jack's coming home. Get ready for him. Make sure the lines are open and the CPU is switched on. See you in cyberspace, kiddo.' I think that was all."

"That's enough. That was Kyle all right. So this is where it's supposed to happen?"

"This," Dan said, "is where it's already happening. Come in. Come in. Better take a deep breath now."

Roy heard the wind's roar before the bedroom door was fully open, but the sight that met his eyes inside was even more dramatic than the sound. At first it seemed that the room was being torn apart by a relentless desert dust storm, but this was more than a storm, and the particles filling the air were more than mere specks of dust. The place was alive with billions of multicolored pixels, a dense, swirling cloud of them. They were so thickly gathered it was hard to tell where they were coming from, but Roy didn't need three good guesses.

The cloud was at its thickest away to his left, where Jack's desk and computer stood. Even through the murk of the pixel-storm, Roy thought he could see a harsh bright light coming from there, a deep chasm in space through which the neon-colors were pouring.

"How long has this been going on?" Alison hollered. The white noise was almost deafening.

"Since I got here." Dan's eyes were wide and wild; he looked like some child who'd been let loose with *Doom* for the first time. "But there's more of a pattern now. It's changing somehow. It's—"

"He's here!" Sandy was screaming. "I can feel him! He's here, I just know it!"

The wind was falling, just as it seemed to do in the Sphere before major changes took place. All through the room, the air was clearing, dot by dot, pixel by pixel. They were amassing now and thickening, merging into some kind of recognizable shape in the area surrounding Jack's desk. Slowly, as Roy watched, open-mouthed, a figure, a ghostly effigy of Jack North, materialized in the space between the office chair and the desk's edge. To begin with, this Jack was little more than a pale imitation, no more substantial than a cloud, yet second by second, more of him snapped into place while numberless electrons still poured from the screen before him.

"I see him," Roy murmured, though no one could have heard him above the wind's roar. He could feel his skin prickling as if he, too, were composed of electronic beams. "I *knew* he was here before, I just knew it."

Dan was laughing, not in amusement but with nervous astonishment, fear, and wonder.

Sandy was making uncontrolled noises, somewhere between airless gasps and full-blown cries. She started toward the desk. As she did so, Alison rushed forward to grab hold of her. "Wait. Wait. Not yet. He isn't complete yet."

Still, he very nearly was. A harsh white light washed through the room, so intense Roy had to shield his eyes momentarily. He could feel the brightness tingling his hands and cheeks like ultra-violet rays; he could sense the presence he'd sensed before, the presence of someone else in the room. As the light fell and he dropped his hands from his eyes, he saw Jack sprawling at the desk, Jack averting his eyes from the dazzling screen, Jack turning to face the crowd at the door.

His hands and face, even his clothing, swarmed with quick nervous ticks. The muscles around his mouth and cheeks were rippling, like those of a pilot undergoing G-force. For a time it seemed his whole body was running out of control. *But his eyes,* Roy thought, *his eyes are telling another story. He knows where he is and what he's doing here. He knows who we are. . . . He's coming home.*

"Didn't you miss me?" Jack said finally. "I thought you'd at least have something to say." Which was when Sandy burst into tears.

214

■   ■   ■

Later, she went down to relay the news to her parents. Upstairs, they kept the door closed. Sandy came back after half an hour, beaming, shaking her head.

"How did they take it?" Jack wanted to know.

"Mum was so happy, she fainted. The doctor is with her. I think she was close to passing out anyway; she's been at the snapping point ever since you've been gone, but she'll be fine now. She'll be up to see you as soon as she can. We'll go down when the reporters have gone. I think they're expecting to hear something, one way or the other. Shall I get rid of them now?"

"Maybe you could ask them to come back tomorrow. For now, just tell them I'm home; that ought to keep them hungry. I have a story to tell, but I'm not ready yet."

"I guess that goes for us, too," Dan said. "What we just saw must've been some kind of freakin' miracle; I *know* you've got a story to tell. Will you tell it to me sometime, too? I wouldn't expect you to now. I'll be moving along soon. I can see you need to rest after what you've been through."

Jack nodded and lay back on his bed, propped up by a mound of soft pillows. "Sure, I'll tell you tomorrow. No. No, wait. I just had a thought."

Sheer instinct made him do what he did then. Leaning forward slightly, he brought one hand up past his shoulder, letting his fingers stray to the small mound of metal embedded at the base of his neck.

"My God," he said on the edge of a breath. He knew almost at once what it was. His head still was a jumble of rushing thoughts, flashes of neon and chrome, but soon it would clear, and then the pieces would fit together. At some point along the journey between Silicon Sphere and here something had changed in him, something deep and private and major. He couldn't be sure yet when the feeling of newness had begun, whether it had started the moment his body became immaterial, transformed into billions of colored pixels, or whether it had been some time before that. There had been moments of terror and doubt, and there were yawning gray chasms where there should have been memories. How *had* he arrived here from the other side? What was the last thing he'd seen before leaving, or the first thing he'd seen on returning? Maybe, in time, it would come back to him. Just now, his mind was still spinning. There was so much to remember, so much to start coming to terms with. "My God, I knew it . . . I just knew it . . ."

"Knew what?" Sandy said. "Knew what?"

"Just a minute. I'll . . . I'll try to explain."

A mound of loose, unused connector cables swarmed on the floor by his desk like snakes. Jack took to his feet, tugged one from the pile, and plugged it neatly into the DAT drive beside the computer. He hesitated, hearing only the thunder of blood between his ears, the beat of his heart like a bass riff. Then, drawing a nervous deep breath, he plugged the other end of the cable into himself.

There now, he thought, breathing out, breathing slowly

216

and evenly. *See how easy that was? How natural—how normal—it felt? Second nature, is what you just did. Second nature. The king of hyperspace has returned with powers beyond his belief.*

Next, he placed a blank tape in the drive. For several seconds the drive's mechanism whirred as Jack transferred the relevant data. Of course he understood the awed gasps and groans the others were making as he did this; of course it would take them time to adjust to the change in him. He still had to adjust to it, too.

"Here you are," he said when he'd finished, ejecting the tape and placing it squarely in Dan's open hands. "That's the whole story. There are sure to be missing pieces, but there's nothing I can tell you now that you won't find right there."

Dan stared at the tape, then at Jack in bewilderment. "This is some kind of practical joke, right? You didn't really do what I thought you just did."

"Take that home and see for yourself," Jack told him. He felt strangely elated, the way he usually felt after riding the roller coaster or fleeing victorious from Zone Eleven to find himself still alive. Seizing an armload of books randomly from the shelf, he struggled to the bedside, dumped the books, began sorting them into two distinct piles: those he had read, those he hadn't.

"You're planning a little light reading?" Roy said.

"Yeah, just a great adventure or two before we eat. Jesus, I'm starving. What time is dinner?"

217